S0-ADG-836

———

She's practically melting against me, and I'm losing my mind. My thoughts reduced to basic, primitive needs, so powerful I can barely stand it.

My condo's only a few blocks away. I could step into the street. Grab a taxi, and take her home.

It would be a bold move. But then again, so was kissing her in an alley.

But, of course, we can't.

———

For all of JK's titles,
please visit www.jkenner.com

LOVELY LITTLE LIAR

J. KENNER

Cover design by Michele Catalano, Catalano Creative

Cover image by Annie Ray/Passion Pages

Digital ISBN: 978-1-940673-97-4

Print ISBN: 978-1-940673-96-7

Published by Martini & Olive

v. 2018-11-5P

CHAPTER ONE

I DON'T BELIEVE in relationships, but I do believe in fucking.

Why, you ask? Hell, I could write a book. *The Guy's Guide to Financial, Emotional, and Business Success.* But honestly, why bother with a book when the thesis boils down to just four words: Don't Date. Just Fuck.

Hear me out.

Relationships take time, and when you're trying to build a business, you need to pour every spare hour into the work. Trust me on this. In the months since my buddies and I launched Blackwell-Lyon Security, we've been busting ass twenty-four/seven. Working assignments, taking meetings, building a rock solid client base.

And our commitment's paying off. I promise you our roster wouldn't be half as full as it is now if I was spending chunks of prime working time answering texts from an insecure girlfriend who was wondering why I wasn't sexting every ten minutes. So skip the dating and watch your business flourish.

Plus, hook-ups don't expect gifts or flowers. Drinks or dinner, maybe, but a guy's gotta eat anyway, right? There may be no such thing as a free lunch, but you can come close to a free fuck.

But it's the emotional upside that's the kicker for me. No walking on eggshells because she's in a bitchy mood. No feeling trapped when she demands to know why poker night was more appealing than watching the latest tearjerker starring some tanned metrosexual sporting a man bun. No wondering if she's banging another guy when she's not answering her texts.

And definitely no falling into a deep, dark pit of gloom when she breaks your engagement two weeks before the wedding because she's not sure she loves you after all.

And no, I'm not bitter. Not anymore.

But I am practical.

The truth is, I like women. The way they laugh. The way they feel. The way they smell.

I get off on making a woman feel good. On making her shatter in my arms and then beg for more.

Like them, yes. But I don't trust them. And I'm not getting fucked over again.

Not like that, anyway.

So there you go. Q.E.D.

I don't do relationships. I do hook-ups. I make it my mission to give every woman who shares my bed the ride of her life.

But it's a one-way street, and I don't go back.

That's just the way I roll. I walked away from relationships a long time ago.

So as I pull up in front of Thyme, the trendy new restaurant in Austin's upscale Tarrytown neighborhood, and hand the valet my keys, all I'm expecting is business as usual. Some causal flirting. A few appetizers. A solid buzz from a little too much liquor. And then a quick jaunt back to my downtown condo for some mid-week action.

What I get instead, is *her*.

CHAPTER TWO

"WELL, then, I need you to make an announcement." The leggy brunette's voice belongs to a woman used to giving orders. "He must be here by now."

Legs is standing in front of me at the hostess stand, her back turned so that all I can see is a mass of chestnut brown waves, a waist small enough for a man to grab onto, and an ass that was made to fill out a skirt. In front of her, a petite blonde clutches a stack of menus like a lifeline as she gnaws on her lower lip.

"Well?" Legs' voice is more demand than question.

While the hostess explains to Legs that the restaurant really isn't set up for announcements, I glance at my watch impatiently. The traffic on Sixth Street had been more of a bitch than usual, and I'm running five minutes late. An irritating reality considering that I'm habitually prompt, a remnant from my military days. I'll cop to a lot of vices, but tardiness isn't among them.

Legs, however, is going to make me even later, and I frown as I glance toward the bar area to my left, looking for any unaccompanied woman who might be "J" from the 2Nite app. But there's no one sitting alone who looks like she's waiting for "PB" to join her.

It's my first time using this particular app, and its schtick—because they all have a schtick—is that all contact is anonymous until you actually meet your date. That's fine and dandy, but it makes connecting difficult. After all, would she really have left her name as J at the hostess desk? Because I'm going to feel like an idiot if I have to call myself PB.

Then again, I'll be lucky to have the chance to call myself anything at all, because Legs is spending so much time harassing the hostess that the restaurant will be closed before I can ask about J or claim a table.

"—except I already told you that I don't have his name," Legs is saying as I tune back into their conversation. The corporate warrior tone has faded, replaced by frustration and, I think, disappointment.

As for the hostess, she now looks even more frazzled.

"All I know is that he works for a security company—"

Ding, ding, ding. Folks, we have a winner.

"—and he should already be here."

"J," I say confidently, stepping up beside her. "I'm Pierce Blackwell." I pull a business card from my wallet and hand it to her when she turns to face me.

"Of Blackwell-Lyon Security. *PB*," I add, just in case that's not absolutely clear. "I'm very happy to meet you in person."

And that, frankly, is one hundred percent true. Because while the rear view might be amazing, from the front, my date for the night is even more stunning. Her dark hair frames a pale face with skin so perfect I have to force myself not to reach out and stroke her cheek. She has a wide mouth that was built for naughty things, and the kind of curvaceous body that lets a man know he has a real woman in his arms.

"Oh." Her voice is a little startled, and her amber eyes are wide with surprise. She's dropped the stern tone she'd used with the hostess, and I see relief in her eyes. I guess she thought I was going to stand her up, despite the fact that she doesn't look like the kind of woman who gets stood up often.

And her obvious relief that I've arrived suggests a vulnerability I wouldn't have guessed from listening to her interrogate the hostess.

Honestly, I like the contrast. It suggests a strong personality wrapped around a soft, feminine core. In other words, a woman who knows what she wants from a man, but isn't afraid to let him take control.

Did I mention I like taking control?

My card is still in her hand, and she glances down as she reads it, her thumb softly rubbing over the raised lettering in what I think must be an unconscious motion, but still makes me imagine the brush of that thumb over my hand, my mouth ... and other much more interesting places.

She lifts her head. And in the moment she meets my eyes, I'm certain that I see a familiar spark. The kind of heat that means we skip the appetizers, slam back a quick get-to-know-you drink, then barely make it back to my condo with clothing intact.

I know women like the way I look. Dark blond hair, a body that's in prime shape at thirty-four thanks to military training and my current job's requirements, plus blue eyes that have been known to draw compliments from strangers.

So the heat I see on her face doesn't surprise me. But

then I blink, and damned if that fire doesn't disappear, her eyes going completely flat. As if someone flipped a switch.

What the hell?

Was I hallucinating? Fantasizing?

Or maybe she's just doing her damnedest to fight an intense, visceral lust.

But why would she? She came here tonight wanting the same thing I did. One night. A good time. And absolutely no strings.

Honestly, it makes no sense. And right now, the only thing I'm certain of is that the desire I saw on her face is gone. *Poof.* Just like a magic trick.

No heat. No fire.

No goddamned interest at all.

"So, will that be two for dinner?" the hostess asks brightly. "The wait's about forty-five minutes in the dining room, but there are a few tables open in the bar."

"That'll be fine," I say, determined to get this evening back on track. "We'll probably stick with drinks and appetizers." I look to her for confirmation, but she's frowning at her phone and doesn't look up again until we're seated.

"The drinks here are good," I say as the hostess leaves us with the bar menus. "I live downtown, so I've been coming here a lot since it opened. How about you? Been here before?"

One perfectly groomed eyebrow arches up in a way that I find incredibly sexy, despite the fact that she's obviously annoyed. "I've only just arrived in town. When would I have had time?"

"Right. Good point." Now I'm just being conciliatory, because how am I supposed to know when she moved to Austin? I read her profile and there wasn't a single word in there about her being new to town. But my only other option is to tell her flat out that tonight is a bust, and then get the hell out of there.

Except I'm not ready to give up on her yet. Because despite our off-kilter start, there's something intriguing about J. And I know damn well that I saw a spark of interest in her eyes. And so help me, I intend to get it back. Because, hey, who doesn't love a challenge?

"Speaking of time," she says. "Under the circumstances, I feel I need to be completely honest."

"Go for it."

"It's just that I didn't appreciate being kept waiting," she says. "Punctuality is extremely important to me."

"Me too." That's true, but I'm surprised she's getting bent out of shape for a mere five minutes. Still, at least we've found one tiny patch of common ground. "I'm almost always early. I'd blame the traffic, but honestly I should have left the office earlier."

I flash my most charming smile. It hasn't failed me yet, and thankfully tonight is no exception. She relaxes a bit and leans back in her chair, her finger tracing the leather edge of the menu.

"I'm glad to hear it. You've seemed lackadaisical about the whole thing so far. It's not the attitude I'm used to."

I reach across the table and take her hand. It's soft and warm, and my cock tightens in response to a fresh wave of lust. She may be prickly and inscrutable, but she's also fiercely self-assured, and the combination is seriously hot.

"Sweetheart," I say. "I may be flippant about a lot of things, but never about this."

"Sweetheart?" She tugs her hand free of mine, and I couldn't have gone limp faster if she'd dunked me in a barrel of ice water. "And you called me *J*, too? I mean, what? Are we starting a hip hop band?"

"We could," I quip, trying to regain my balance. "PB and J. You have to admit it works."

I laugh, because it *does* work. And why the hell is she griping at me, anyway? If using initials irritates her that much, she should have picked an app other than 2Nite.

"Just call me Jez," she says. "Or Ms. Stuart if you prefer to be more formal." She's sitting up straight now, and I'm thinking that she couldn't be more formal if she tried.

"Jez," I say. "I like it."

"It's short for Jezebel, obviously. And of course our parents named my sister along the same theme." She leans back, clearly expecting a response.

"Parents will do that," I say, since I've got nothing else. Let's just say that talk of parents and siblings isn't usually par for the course on these kinds of dates.

Still, it must have been the right thing to say, because she smiles, and it's the kind of smile that lights her whole face. And even though I don't do full nights—not ever—I can't help thinking that it's the kind of smile I'd like to wake up to.

"Listen," she says, "I know I may seem formal and demanding, and that can be a little off-putting for some people. It's just that I take all of this very, very seriously."

"I get that." I mean what I say. After all, I know that I'm a nice guy, but a woman has to be careful who she goes home with.

"I'm glad you understand," she says as the waiter comes up to take our order.

I hand the waiter my menu. "Angel's Envy. On the rocks. And the lady will have...?"

"Club soda with lime." She meets my eyes as the waiter walks away. "I like to keep a clear head."

Okay, sparks or not, this woman is exasperating. "Honestly, right now, I'm thinking I should have ordered a double."

Her mouth tightens with disapproval. "Fine. But I hope you have a clear head when it counts. I expect complete attention to detail."

I hold her gaze for ten full seconds. And then—because at this point I have nothing to lose—I slowly let my eyes roam down. Her usually full lips, now pressed together in a thin red line. The soft curve of her jaw. The tender slope of her neck.

Her top button of her silk blouse has come open, and I can see the curve of her breasts spilling out over the cups of her pale pink bra. I pause just long enough to imagine the taste of her right there. The feel of her soft skin against my lips. And the way her bossy, severe voice will soften when she writhes beneath me and begs for more.

Slowly, I raise my eyes. "Sweetheart," I say. "I'm all about the details."

I watch, satisfied, as a pink stain colors her cheeks. She exhales, then swallows. "Right. Well, that's good."

I bite back a smile. I'm not sure what kind of game we've been playing, but there's no doubt in my mind that the score is currently in my favor.

She draws a breath, and I can tell she's trying to gather herself. "So if you're all about the details, then you already know my problem."

I lean back, grateful when the waiter returns with my drink, as that gives me time to think. *Problem?* The only problem I remember her mentioning in her profile was that she'd been working such long hours she hadn't been properly laid in months. I'd assured her I could remedy that, and she'd promptly accepted my RFD—which is 2Nite speak for "request for date."

"Well, you've been going a hundred miles an hour," I say, and she nods, looking pleased that I remember.

"And all this drama with my sister is adding a whole new layer of insanity."

"Your sister?"

She looks at me sharply, and I immediately, regret my words.

"I thought you'd done your homework." There's a challenge in her voice, but I barely notice it. I'm too mesmerized by the way her lips now close over her straw.

I shift, my jeans feeling uncomfortably snug. And honestly, what the hell? Because I can already tell this woman is bad news. Intriguing, maybe. Challenging, definitely. But way, way too much trouble.

Apparently, the parts of me below the table aren't nearly as critical, however. But I'm going to attribute that to a general desire to get laid, and not necessarily to Jez.

"Well?" she presses.

"Are you always this..." I trail off, thinking better of saying what I was thinking. *Bitchy.*

"What?"

"It's just that this smells remarkably like a job interview. Which seems a bit like overkill for just one night."

"One night? Oh, no. I'm looking for something for at least three weeks. After that, we can decide if a long term commitment would make sense."

"Wait. What?"

"I was with Larry for over five years," she says, which explains why she's been so awkward tonight. I'm guessing this is her first time to even use a dating app.

"That's quite a while," I say.

"It is. And honestly, I prefer the continuity that goes with a long-term arrangement. With someone I can trust, of course. That's what I'll be evaluating with you, of course. Assuming you check out and can prove yourself. Which, frankly, I'm starting to doubt."

I wince, suddenly picturing a panel of Olympic judges at the foot of my bed as I attempt a double rolling dismount with a flip.

I shake my head, dismissing the thought.

"Right. Okay. Let's back up." I slam back the rest of my bourbon. "Now it's my turn to call you out for being unprepared. Because my profile is crystal clear. No long term commitments." I flash that charming smile again. "Forget marriage. I'm all about the one-night stand."

"That's absurd. You're seriously considering doing this for just one night? And you think that would be okay with me? That I want to do this repeatedly?" She gestures at the table, as if having a man buy you a drink is the most hideous torture imaginable. "Are you insane?"

"My shrink doesn't think so."

She stands, then hooks her purse over her shoulder. "I wish your policy had been made clear. This has been a complete waste of time in a week when I don't have any time to waste."

"Jez—" I stand and reach for her, but she steps back. I have no idea why I want her to stay, but I do.

She, however, isn't giving me the chance to convince her.

"Thank you for the drink." She draws a breath, and I can see her effort to settle herself. "I really am sorry for the misunderstanding. Despite everything, I think it would have been... *interesting* working with you."

And then she turns.

And then she's gone.

What the hell just happened?

"Another?" the waiter asks, as I sink back into my chair.

"Yeah. A double this time. I think I need it."

I sit there for a minute, a little shell-shocked, and I'm not sure why. I damn sure shouldn't be disappointed she walked, because that one would have been trouble for sure. The last thing I need is a woman who wants to cling.

But still, I've sat in a bar and had a drink by myself on several occasions. But never before has the empty seat across from me seemed quite so empty.

I sigh, then lift the drink the waiter slides in front of me. I savor the bite of the whiskey, wondering if it's the alcohol that's messing with my head. Making me think that maybe two dates wouldn't be the end of the world. Hell, maybe even three.

Because the truth is, even though I never quite figured her out, I haven't been that entertained by a woman in a long time.

My phone chirps, signaling an incoming message from 2Nite.

I snatch it from my jacket pocket, certain it's a message from Jez.

But it's not.

Oh, it's from J, all right. But as I read it, I get a dark, twisting feeling in my gut.

Sorry I missed our date. Work blew up and I had to fly to Dallas. Rain check?

J

I read it twice, just to make sure that the bourbon isn't making me hallucinate.

But, no. The message is clear. J—the woman I was all set

to meet here tonight—isn't in Austin. She's two hundred miles away.

Which means that she didn't show.

Which means that Jez isn't J.

Which means that I have no idea who Jezebel Stuart is.

And I damn sure don't know what the hell we spent the evening talking about.

CHAPTER THREE

I SIT in the bar and nurse my drink for a full fifteen
minutes before lightning finally strikes, and I get it. And,
yeah, maybe I should have made sense of the whole convo-
luted mess faster, but my head wasn't in the game. Instead,
it was on those never-ending legs. That soft skin. Those
sultry, penetrating eyes.

Not to mention a mouth that was made for both sin and
sarcasm.

I'd been distracted, yes. And more than a little slow on
the uptake. But I give myself credit for pulling it together at
the end. And the moment I do—the moment I finally understand the complete and total clusterfuck that was our
conversation—I bolt out of my chair and head for the door.

Jez, of course, is long gone.

Damn.

I head back inside and drop into the chair I'd aban-
doned. My watered down drink is still there, although the
bus boy's about to grab it. I practically growl at him, like an
alpha lion claiming the last scrap of a downed gazelle, and
he backs away, eyes wide.

I slam back the dregs of my drink, then chew on the ice as I tap my phone thoughtfully.

Now that I see the big picture, the real scenario is painfully obvious. I'd come here expecting to meet my hook-up. She'd come expecting to hire some unreliable cop-in-a-box who hadn't showed.

Or had he?

I frown, pondering the coincidence. Had he? More specifically, had *I* showed?

With a groan, I lean back in my chair, and take a deep whiff. Because right now, I'm afraid I smell a rat.

I pull out my phone, dial Kerrie's home number, and wait for her to pick up.

"Don't I get enough of you at work?" my sister says.

"You can never get enough of me, and you know it."

She snorts. "Seriously, what's up? I'm running a bath, and there's a sexy Scottish laird waiting for me to join him."

"Anticipation," I say. "Makes everything all the sweeter." Our mother had a collection of Barbara Cartland novels that my little sister discovered when she was eleven and I was twenty-one. She was my parents' surprise-it's-not-really-menopause-yet baby, and because of that she spent more time hanging around the house as a kid than I had. My parents were older and working and less inclined to drive her all over creation, and I was in the Middle East for my first tour, and not around to play big brother.

Apparently Dame Cartland is a gateway drug, because I'm pretty sure that Kerrie has now read every romance novel ever written. All of them, that is, except for ones featuring ex-Special Forces heroes. She says she pictures me and that it's just too weird.

"Especially since you're hardly romance hero material,"

she once quipped. And considering that a romance requires more connection than a late night hook-up, she's probably right.

Now she sighs dramatically. "What do you need?"

"Did you schedule a meeting between me and a woman named Jezebel Stuart?"

"Wait—what?" Her voice is sharp now, interested, and I'm certain that she's my culprit.

"Dammit, Kerrie. If you schedule an appointment, you have to push it through to the calendar. That's about as basic as your job gets."

"I know how to do my damn job, and I didn't schedule an appointment with you. But—"

"With Cayden? Connor?" I rattle off my partners' names.

"No. No appointment. Nada. Zip. Now do you want to drop the bullshit and tell me what's going on?"

"Are you at your computer?"

"Yes, I have a computer in my bathroom." I can practically hear her roll her eyes. "What do you need?"

"I want some background on this woman. Jezebel—"

"Stuart. Yeah, I know. You said. I don't need a computer for that. She's from Phoenix, but she's lived in LA for the last ten years. She's in Texas right now, though. Her sister's filming a movie. And why am I telling you all this?"

"Are you already online? How do you know all that?"

"Um, maybe because I have a life and read things other than *Tactical Weapons* and *Security Magazine.*"

"And *Peanuts,*" I add dryly. "I never miss Snoopy in the Sunday paper."

"Her sister's Delilah Stuart," she continues, ignoring me. "And Jezebel's her manager. Is that why they're hiring us? Because of all the harassment Delilah's been getting since she cheated on Levyl with Garreth Todd?"

"Not exactly." I have no idea who Levyl is, but I'm familiar with Garreth Todd. Mostly because all of my spare time isn't spent buried in my magazines, despite what my sister thinks. I also have a deep affection for any movie with a high body count and at least one kickass car chase, and Todd has starred in three of my recent favorites.

As a general rule, I'd rather shove bamboo under my fingernails than read, discuss, or think about Hollywood gossip. But now that Kerrie's brought it up, I do remember a conversation a while back. A date of mine kept droning on about some former child actress who'd recently skyrocketed to superstardom as an adult. At first, she'd been beloved by fans. Not only because of her breakout role, but because she was dating the lead singer of a popular boy band. The kind of band whose songs send tween girls into convulsive fits and have grown women secretly buying unauthorized biographies in the grocery store checkout line.

Apparently, the actress and the singer's romance played out in the tabloids, with the two being a sugary-sweet power couple that everyone rooted for.

But then the actress was awarded a plum part in a major movie opposite Garreth Todd. When the news broke that the actress had slept with Todd—thus breaking the singer's heart—she immediately went from being America's sweetheart to being a soulless harpy who shredded men's lives. She was still making the front page of entertainment magazines, but now it was because she was reviled and hated by females the world over, all of whom were taking the singer's broken heart way, way, way too personally.

As far as I know, there were no death threats against the

actress, but considering my date's vitriol when she relayed the whole soap opera to me, I wouldn't be surprised.

My date had ended the story by saying the actress got what she deserved. Apparently, she'd been fired from some big franchise movie, and was pretty much a pariah as far as getting a job was concerned.

Like I said, a soap opera.

At the time, the actress's name meant nothing to me. Now, I'm certain it was Delilah Stuart.

Before I get the chance to ask Kerrie for more details, she plows on. "This is going to be great. I bet Delilah has all sorts of security assignments coming down the pipe. And if we have her business, we can get more entertainment jobs. There's so much film and music work in Austin, and even with all the controversy, a recommendation from Delilah would be golden. We could totally plug the hole left by Talbot, you know?"

I did know. Blackwell-Lyon is still a relatively new business, and when the guys and I broke off from our old firm we'd anticipated a steady stream of contracts with Reginald Talbot, a Silicon Valley billionaire who moved his family and his business to Austin about ten years ago. But five months after Blackwell-Lyon opened its doors, Talbot decided to retire, sold the entirety of his operation to some huge corporation, and headed to the Mediterranean with his wife.

In other words, he's working on his tan, and my partners and I are scrambling to fill the gap in our client base.

"So what exactly happened?" Kerrie asked. "You had a meeting with her? How?"

"Irrelevant," I say, because once Kerrie knows the real story, I'll never hear the end of it. "Right now, I just need to find out where she's staying." I'm a security expert, not a PI.

But over the years, I've cultivated some resources. "Call Gordo and tell him I have a rush job."

"Please would be nice."

"Please."

"Well, since you asked so nicely..."

"Kerrie." There's a warning in my voice.

"I'm just messing with you. I don't need to call Gordo. Delilah's staying at the Violet Crown. So I bet Jezebel is, too."

"And you know this how?" I ask, already mentally calculating how long it will take to drive there. The Violet Crown is a high-end boutique hotel in central Austin. And, conveniently, just a few miles away from Thyme.

"Twitter. Someone at the hotel snapped her picture and posted it. *Hashtag Delilah Stuart.*"

I frown. "When was it posted? Are there others?"

She's obviously at her computer now, because I hear her tapping keys. "Um, the post went up about fifteen minutes ago. And it's got a couple of dozen likes." There's more tapping. "But I don't see any more posts. Lots of retweets, though. Why?"

I ignore the question. "I'll call you later." I've left a fifty on the table, and I'm already on my way to the valet stand.

"Pierce," she presses as I pass my ticket to the valet. "What's going on?"

"Nothing, I hope."

"But—"

I hang up, then drum my finger on the ledge of the valet stand. I want my car, and with every second that passes the knot in the pit of my stomach cinches just a little tighter.

I may not have the full story yet, but I know enough.

I know that Jez came to Thyme because she was looking

to hire a security detail. I know she mentioned her sister in our conversation.

I know that Delilah's still reviled by fans.

And I know that her location is now public.

Call me paranoid, but that doesn't sit well with me.

CHAPTER FOUR

"I NEED you to connect me to Jezebel Stuart's room." I'm racing down Fifth Street toward Lamar Boulevard, my phone hooked up to the Range Rover's audio system.

Hopefully, I'm worrying about nothing. Surely the current production company has security on Delilah. But if so, then why was Jezebel looking to hire me? Or, rather, why was she looking to hire the guy who was supposed to have shown up instead of me?

I don't know, and at the moment, I don't care. Bottom line, Jez may think I'm a total incompetent prick, but I can't walk away until I'm certain she and her sister are safe.

"I'm sorry, sir, but there's no one by that name registered here." The girl doesn't sound like she's old enough to legally drink, and I know that I'm ruining her day. But better hers than Jezebel's.

"Excellent," I say, adding a little charm to my voice. "That's exactly how you were supposed to respond. I'll be sure and let your manager know that you've stuck with protocol."

I pause long enough to let her tell me that she has no

idea what I'm talking about. When she stays silent, I know I guessed right: Jez and Delilah are guests, management is fully aware, and the staff has been ordered to protect their privacy no matter what.

"I'm with the studio's publicity department. Jezebel's expecting my call."

"But I'm not supposed to put anyone through."

"No, you're not," I say. "And I commend you for being so diligent. You were informed of the call in protocol, I assume?"

"Um—"

"My apologies, you should have been made fully aware. Obviously we have to be able to get through to the Stuarts, even if they've turned off their cell phones. So you just put me on hold, then call up. Tell Jezebel that Pierce Blackwell needs to speak to her. *PB*," I add. "Be sure to tell her it's PB. And tell her it's important."

I'm pretty sure my name isn't going to win any points with Jez. But I'm hoping she'll pick up the call out of sheer curiosity.

"But—"

"That's the designated procedure," I insist as I make a right turn onto Lamar and head toward the bridge. "Once Ms. Stuart accepts, you just need to patch through this call."

"Oh. Okay. Hold please."

Elevator music starts to play, and I give myself a mental high five.

My victory fades quickly, however, as my time on hold extends. I'm at the bridge. I'm on the bridge. Now I'm stuck at a light. I glance to my right at the moon reflecting on the surface of the river that we locals called Town Lake until the city renamed it Lady Bird Lake about a decade ago. It's a dammed off section of the Colorado River, and why we don't just call it that is one of life's little mysteries.

I let my eyes travel up to the low, rolling hills on the south side of the river. I can't see it from this angle, but I know the Violet Crown's up there. And Jezebel.

By the time I'm over the bridge and making a right turn onto Barton Springs Road, I'm still on hold, and I'm thinking that Jez has shut me down entirely, and I'll never get through.

I'm about to end the call, re-dial, and try again, when the clerk comes back on the line. "I'll connect you now," she says, before I can ask what happened.

And then it's Jez's voice. "How did you find me? For that matter, why are you calling? Did I leave something at the bar?"

"I'm about three minutes from your hotel. I'm going to pull in behind the hotel and park by the service entrance. A black Range Rover. Get your stuff. Get your sister, and meet me back there."

"In case it escaped your notice, you and I don't work together."

"If you're always this argumentative, I'll take that as a good thing. But right now, you need to trust me. I'm moving you to a different location."

"Trust you? I don't even know you. For that matter, I'm pretty sure I don't like you."

"Only pretty sure? Glad to know there's a small window I can crawl through."

"Pierce—"

"And maybe you don't like me, but you do trust me," I continue. "If you didn't, you wouldn't have taken my call at all. So I'm betting you checked me out. Went to my website. Googled my company, my background."

She says nothing, which I take as confirmation.

"Where's Delilah?" I ask, careful to keep my victory smile out of my voice.

"I thought you didn't know anything about my sister?"

"I'm a quick study. And I know that someone tweeted your hotel."

"*Shit.*"

Her tone makes it clear that she didn't know. "You should have some sort of set-up for alerts," I say mildly.

"I do—or I did." She curses softly again. "It's just that lately there's been so much on the Internet about Delilah that my phone never stopped dinging. Now our publicist pulls it nightly and emails it to me every morning."

"Look, the Crown's a great little hotel, but it's not secure enough for you. Get your sister, meet me, and let me take you someplace safe."

"Why is this even your problem?"

And that, I think, is a very good question. And one I'm not sure how to answer. Primarily because the real answer—that she's filled my head, and not helping her is simply unacceptable—is something I don't want to acknowledge. Much less share.

So instead I go with an honest lie. Something true, but not my reason. "Because I think you and I have something in common," I say.

"I sincerely doubt it."

"I have a younger sister," I say. "And I'd move heaven and earth to make sure nothing bad happened to her."

For a moment, she says nothing. Then she says very softly, "She's not here. They had a late call tonight. One of the guys working set security is bringing her back. But she texted me a few minutes ago. They're close."

I've reached the Crown now. It's low and sprawling and

shaped like a U, the interior of which sports a popular—and public—open-air bar that surrounds a pool.

All of the rooms have patios that look out over either the pool or the greenbelt. A valet stand is at the apex of the circular drive, right at the access point to the bar area. I'm guessing that Delilah made the mistake of stepping onto her patio or in front of a window, and a fan snapped a picture from the bar area.

The valet stand is also right by the main entrance to the hotel's interior, which is accessed by a short covered walkway that runs in front of the bar area to a door at the end of one of the U's prongs. Which means that anyone coming into the hotel has to walk past the bar. Which is great for generating business. But not great for privacy or security.

As I drive slowly forward, I can see that the bar is teeming. It's always been popular, but right now it's so full of bodies it looks like Dante's version of hell.

I'm hoping that the place instituted a really amazing Wednesday night Happy Hour, and that accounts for the crowd. But I'm thinking that some of those people came not for the drinks, but for the entertainment. And Delilah, I'm afraid, is the star attraction.

"Text your sister. Have the driver take her around back."

"Too late," she says. "She says they just pulled up."

Sure enough, a black Lincoln Town Car has rolled to a stop right past the valet stand. The bellboy must recognize the car, because he scurries to open the back passenger side door. The driver gets out, and starts to circle around to the passenger side as well.

I can't see who's in the car, but the crowd in the bar has a clear view, and as soon as the door opens, a throng of them stand. I've rolled down my windows, and the catcalls and cries of *bitch* and *slut* and *Levyl deserves better* ring loud and clear.

I slam the car into gear and plow forward just as the crowd starts throwing rotten tomatoes. And half a dozen cameras flash intermittently, illuminating the scene.

The tomatoes splatter on the sidewalk, and Delilah dives back into the car, slamming the door shut behind her as a hail storm of little red bombs explode against the side of the car.

I bring the Rover to a squealing stop beside the Lincoln. "What's happening?" Jezebel cries, her voice tinny through the speakers.

I don't bother answering. I'm out of the car and pulling open the left-side passenger door on the Lincoln. Delilah, looking young and scared, cowers away from me. I hold out my hand. "I'm with Jez. Come on."

She hesitates, and I'm thinking that I'm going to have to dive in the car and forcibly scoop her up, when Jez's voice blares from the Range Rover's speakers. "Do what he says, Del. I'm coming."

Immediately, Delilah lunges for me. I grab her hand and pull her toward me, then load her into the back seat of the Range Rover.

"Hey!" the security guy calls, solidifying my assessment of him as an incompetent prick.

On the hotel side of the Lincoln, a group of women are surging forward, their eyes filled with an anger I don't understand, but certainly can't deny.

"*Bitch!*"

"*Levyl was too good for you!*"

"*How could you hurt him like that?*"

"*Whore!*"

They're getting closer, and I'm on my way back to the driver's side, yelling for Jez to meet us at the service entrance.

But right as I'm about to get into the car, she bursts through the hotel door, then skids to a halt, just a few feet from the boiling crowd. *Shit.*

Her phone's at her ear, and I can hear her cry of, "Delilah!" in stereo—from the sidewalk a few yards away, and through the rolled-down window of my Range Rover.

"Jez!" Delilah calls. "Please, mister!"

I hesitate only a second, debating whether it would be faster to get in the Rover or sprint to the sidewalk.

I sprint.

The crowd's not interested in her at first, but then someone calls out, *Jezebel*, and they move *en masse* toward her, shouting questions about Delilah. A surge of furious energy rips through me—they are *not* touching her—and I push myself to get to her faster, only taking an easy breath when I finally grab her outstretched hand.

"Come on," I order, even though there's no need. She's right beside me and we race toward the car together, fingers twined, while young women grab at my jacket, shouting curses and questions and swearing that Delilah will pay for the way she hurt their sweet, wonderful Levyl.

"In," I say, opening the door so she can get in behind me and be next to her sister. I slam the door, climb into the car, and burn rubber getting back to the street.

I don't stop until we're well away from the hotel. Then I pull into one of the lots at Zilker Park, cut the engine, and relax, my eyes going immediately to the rear view mirror. To *her.*

The women are right next to each other, Jez's arms around Delilah, who's cuddled up against her, crying softly.

After a moment, Jez lifts her eyes and meets mine in the mirror. *Thank you*, she mouths, and I look away, my chest tightening with emotion. I tell myself I'm only thinking about Kerrie. Putting myself in Jez's shoes, and empathizing about how she's feeling now that her sister's safe.

It's not true, of course. What I'm feeling is the shock of this woman's gratitude. That soft, grateful look from a woman I know is strong and competent, but who still needed me. And the pride of coming through for her.

For her.

Because it's not about the job. It's about the woman. And that's not something I've felt in a long time.

Frankly, it's not something I want to feel at all.

Suddenly, the huge interior of my Range Rover is feeling claustrophobic. I grab the handle and open the door, then step out, shutting it behind me. They need privacy. And I need space.

But after a few minutes, I hear the door open, then slam shut. I'm leaning against the front of the Rover, looking out toward the soccer field and the river. My condo's on the other side, and from this angle, I can see the rise of my building blending in with the downtown Austin skyline.

Home.

"It's a pretty view," Jez says, easing up beside me. "Your first time in Austin, right?"

I'm still looking at the city lights, but I can see her in my periphery. The way she turns toward me, her head tilted just slightly, as if I'm a knotty puzzle she has to solve. "Why were you at Thyme? It wasn't to meet me."

"Blind date," I say, turning toward her. "Mistaken identity." I nod toward the car. "We should write it up. It could be one of those romantic caper films. Your sister could star."

Immediately, her expression shuts down and she wraps

her arms around herself as if cold. It's March, but it's Austin, so there's barely a chill in the air. Even so, I take off my jacket and put it around her shoulders. She flashes me a quick smile, looking both sheepish and vulnerable. "I'm starting to wonder if there's going to be anything to star in."

"What are you talking about?"

For a moment, I think she's going to answer. Then the wall slams back in place, and she just shakes her head. "Nothing. Never mind."

"Jez..."

"Honestly, it's not your problem." She pushes away from the car. "Thanks for your help—really. But we'll be fine now. When you take us back, you should probably go to that service entrance, though."

"We're not going back," I say.

"Excuse me?"

"It's South By Southwest right now," I tell her, referring to the well-attended Austin conference and festival. "We're talking fans, reporters, the whole nine yards. They're all in town. And the Violet Crown isn't secure. You think the photographers are going to stay away from that bar just because you ask them nicely?"

"You're right," she says, surprising me. "I'll take care of it tomorrow."

"How about we take care of it tonight?"

Her lips press tight together. "I appreciate what you did," she says. "But I'm not hiring you. I need a firm that can provide a long-term solution, not a one-night fix."

"Tonight's working out pretty well for you," I say with a wry grin. "But just to be clear, in work, I'm all about long-term relationships."

"So it's just your personal life that's truncated?"

Something about the way she says it stabs me in the gut.

As if she's stripped me down to the essentials and found me wanting. "Yeah," I say. "I've slipped on the relationship suit before. It's a little too tight for my taste."

She nods. "Well, I don't suppose it matters either way. We're not in a relationship, we're not having a one-night stand, and I already have a new security team lined up for the rest of the shoot."

"Led by the same guy who didn't show up at Thyme?"

"Actually, yeah."

I nod. "Seems reliable and solid. Good choice."

"The studio vetted him," she says tightly. "They just got the date wrong when they set up the meet. He's flying in tomorrow."

"And Larry?"

Her brow furrows. "What about Larry?"

"He's your former security detail, right? The one you were with for five years?" I make a spinning motion with my finger beside my head. "I reran our conversation in my head. It makes a lot more sense now that I know who you weren't."

"What about him?"

"He approve of your new guy?"

"I—I wouldn't know." She draws a breath and looks down at the ground. "He died over a year ago. A drunk driver in Newport Beach."

My blood pounds through me—this story is too familiar. "Larry?" I say. "Laurence Piper?" Colonel Laurence Piper?"

Her eyes widen. "You knew him?"

"I spent six months under him. I went to his funeral," I add.

"You were in Special Forces."

I nod. I don't like to talk about my time in uniform. I

don't regret it—I have my job and my training because of the skills I learned in the military—but the things I saw can haunt a man. And I learned a long time ago to turn my back on the pain.

"I think Larry would want me to make sure you're safe," I say now. "To get you out of the Crown." The wind's blown a strand of hair over her lips, and I brush it away without thinking, surprised by the shock of awareness that jolts through me as my fingers brush her cheek.

She feels it, too. I'm certain of it. I hear her shuddering breath. I see the way she drops her gaze, then starts to take a step back. She stops herself, pulling my jacket tighter around her. When she looks up again, she's all business. "We'll never find a room. It's the festival, remember? And all of our stuff is at the Crown."

"In other words, if I can get your things delivered to you and set you up in a room, you'll move hotels, no argument?"

"Well, hell," she says. "I walked into that one."

I fight a smug grin. "Right straight into the fire."

Her lips are pressed together, but this time it's not with irritation, but because she's trying not to laugh. And the effort is making her eyes light up, giving her a glow that's both sexy and sweet ... and really not the direction my thoughts need to be traveling.

After a second, she pulls herself together. "Okay. Fine. You win. But you'll never get a room. It's insanity."

"Shall we bet?" Now I'm the one playing with fire. But I can't help it. I want to feel the heat, even at the risk of being burned.

Her eyes narrow. "What are the stakes?"

"I thought you were my date earlier tonight. Let's make it official. Have dinner with me tomorrow."

A single brow rises in that way she has. "When you thought I was your date, we were having drinks."

"Fair enough," I say. "Drinks and appetizers. Deal?"

"Deal," she says. "But you're not going to win."

"Watch me." I pull out my phone, hoping my confidence isn't misplaced, then dial a friend I haven't spoken to in years. "Ryan Hunter," I tell her. "He used to own his own security business, but now he's the Security Chief for Stark International," I continue, referencing the huge international conglomerate owned by former tennis-pro turned billionaire entrepreneur, Damien Stark.

"And that's helpful how?"

"The new Starfire Hotel on Congress Avenue is a Stark property. So if management is holding back a room, I'm ninety percent sure Ryan can snag it for me."

He answers on the fourth ring, and after some quick catching up, I cut to the chase. "Ideally a suite," I say after explaining the situation. "But I'd be grateful for anything you can wrangle."

"Hang on," he says, then puts me on hold. "You're in," he says when he returns. "Ask for Luis when you get there. He'll get them set up."

"I owe you."

"I'll remember that."

I chuckle, then hang up. A lot of the security business is run on traded favors. Today, that practice worked well for me—and for Jez, who's eyeing me with curiosity.

I flash a victorious smile. "Never bet against the house."

"Let's go," she says, and though her voice is stern, I hear the humor underneath.

As promised, Luis takes good care of Del and Jez, providing them with pseudonyms for check-in, a suite on a floor with private key access, and a floor plan that consists of two bedrooms that connect from opposite sides to a huge living area.

"I hope this is suitable?" Luis asks.

"It's great," Jez assures him.

"So you're all set," I say after Luis leaves. He's promised to personally act as a liaison with the Crown to arrange the delivery of both women's things. "Tomorrow night. I'll pick you up at eight."

"I'll meet you at Thyme," she says, then smiles innocently.

"Fair enough. But no club soda with lime."

"Deal," she says.

"You two need to shake on it," Delilah says, walking in from the bedroom she'd claimed.

I hadn't gotten much of a look at her earlier, but it's easy to see why she'd shot to stardom. At eighteen, she has a maturity about her that seems much older. But there's an innocence, too, suggesting a life that's just a little too sheltered.

She's shorter than her sister, and thinner. Almost too thin, at least for my taste.

Her face is classically beautiful, but a smattering of freckles gives her an approachable quality. She's full of laughter, despite the harassment by the fans, and it's easy to tell which is the more serious of the sisters.

"Thank you again," Delilah says to me, for what must be the thousandth time. "For the rescue and for the room."

"You're welcome again," I say, and she grins.

"He was good, wasn't he?" she says to Jez.

"Bossy and arrogant," Jez says, her eyes flickering to me. "But, yeah. He was good."

I smile, more pleased than I should be by the compliment.

"Of course, he's also an ass," she adds, making Delilah burst into laughter.

"Watch it, or I'll make another bet. I think we both know your track record."

"I'm quaking with terror."

Delilah's head moves, her eyes wide as she watches the two of us like a tennis game. "So tomorrow, right? I'll just hang out here."

"You'll definitely hang out here," Jez says. "No late shoot tomorrow. So no repeat of tonight." She glances at her watch. "You have a five a.m. call. I'll wake you at four. Go." She nods toward the bedroom.

Delilah looks at me, her expression exasperated. "She forgets that it's been five years since I was thirteen."

"You forget what a bitch you are when you don't get enough sleep."

That's her, Delilah mouths, holding up a hand to shield the finger she's pointing at Jez.

"I heard that."

"I'm going, I'm going." Delilah pauses in the door of her room. "Thanks again, Pierce. For everything."

"My pleasure," I say. And then she closes her door, and I'm alone with Jez, and this palatial suite seems suddenly too small.

I clear my throat. "I should let you get to sleep, too."

She nods. "Yeah. It's late."

"Tomorrow," I say.

"Tomorrow." She steps toward me, and my heart pounds in anticipation of her touch—and then with mortification when I realize that all she's doing is walking to the door.

"Lock it behind me," I order.

"Of course."

Then I'm outside, and she smiles, and the door closes in my face.

And that, I think, is the end of that.

Except it's not. I'm going to see her tomorrow.

And right then I realize that I made a mistake with that bet. I should have kept my mouth shut.

I should have just walked away.

Because Jezebel Stuart is the kind of woman who gets under your skin.

But I'm not the kind of man who sticks.

CHAPTER FIVE

"THIS IS MY FAVORITE SHOT," Kerrie says, holding up her tablet so that Connor can see what she's looking at. Then she turns it to me, as if I'm just an afterthought. "I like how everything's in focus except you and Delilah. You're both just a little blurry."

"Nice," I say, leaning back against the break room countertop and sipping my second cup of late-afternoon coffee. After a day reviewing blueprints in prep for an upcoming job, I need the caffeine. "Way to be kind to your big brother."

The image is from the Crown, and it shows Delilah and me hurrying from the Town Car to my Range Rover.

"An action shot," Connor says, flashing a wide grin. "And with a movie star. I don't know, Blackwell. Could be the start of a whole new career for you."

"Nah," my sister says to Connor. "You're the one with the movie star looks."

"Hey." I hold up my hands, pretending offense. "What am I? Dog food?"

She sets the tablet down and eyes me critically. "You'll

do," she says. "Empirically you're pretty hot, even if you are my brother. It's the eyes that do it. You have bedroom eyes."

By the fridge, Connor snorts.

"I'm serious," my sister says. "I mean, he's got the body for sure—thank you Uncle Sam— and a solid jawline. Extra points, by the way, for the beard stubble."

"I try."

"But it's those pale blue eyes that get him laid. I mean, basically he got what I was supposed to have. The bastard."

My sister has dark hair and brown eyes, and she knows damn well that she's stunning.

"But *you*," she continues, looking to Connor, "you have that mysterious dark thing going on. It's seriously hot."

"You just want in my bed," Connor teases.

"Been there, done that," she says airily.

As always whenever their past fling comes up, I eye both of them, searching for signs that their short-lived relationship is going to somehow blow up—and blow back on the business. But they both seem fine with having moved on. And although that surprises me—Kerrie's had a crush on Connor since she was thirteen and I brought him and Cayden home with me when we were on leave— I also know that the fourteen-year age difference between them is something that Connor was never comfortable with.

Since they didn't bother consulting me when they broke it off, I don't know all the reasons. But I do know they've stayed friends.

Which works out well for the business, because my sister's doing a stellar job as our office manager, a role she took on after she confessed to me that she was bored out of her mind with her previous job as a paralegal. Now, she runs the office and is going to school part time for her MBA.

She picks up the tablet again. "There are dozens more pictures like that one. Maybe hundreds. Want to see?"

"No," I say firmly, as Connor says, "Hell, yes."

"Fine," she says, putting the tablet down with a smirk. "I'll show Connor later, when Cayden's here to share your humiliation."

"That's why you're my favorite sister. You treat me so well."

"I'm amazing," she chirps. "But seriously, your fifteen minutes of fame could be good for our bottom line."

Cayden slides into the room, then leans against the wall, his arms crossed. "Well, that's something I like to hear. What did our Mr. Blackwell do?"

Kerrie passes him the tablet, then gives him a rundown of last night—her version, at least. Cayden listens, amused, his expression much the same as Connor's. To be expected, I suppose. They're identical twins. But it's easy to tell them apart these days. Cayden wears a patch over his left eye— the injury being the reason he'd been discharged three years ago despite intending to stay in the game until retirement.

He still does some fieldwork at Blackwell-Lyon, but mostly he's the face of our organization. And he's damn good at the job. "The patch makes me look tough," he often says. "And that's a baseline requirement when I'm asking folks to put their lives in our hands."

He hands the tablet back to Kerrie. "So all this coverage is bringing in new business?"

"Not a flood," she says. "But I must have fielded at least a half-dozen calls today. I guess folks figure if Pierce is watching out for Delilah, then he can watch out for them, too."

"She hired us?" Cayden asked, which was a very Cayden-like way to cut to the chase.

"No," I say. "That was a one-off."

"You never did tell me how you met them," Kerrie says.

"I met Jezebel at Thyme. We'd both been stood up."

"Mmm." I can tell she doesn't believe me. I can live with that.

"All that good work and she didn't hire you?" Connor asks. "What kind of a rainmaker are you?"

"The kind who's not." It's no secret that my skills are in the field. Cultivating new business is Cayden's specialty. "But all things considered, I think I did all right." I point at Kerrie. "Didn't she just say the phone's been ringing all day? I've done my job."

I keep my tone light. A *nothing to see here, move along folks* kind of attitude.

But the truth? The truth is I do want the job. Because without it, tonight's going to be the last time I see Jezebel Stuart. And that small fact isn't sitting well with me at all.

"Okay, enough about my brother. Are we gonna have this meeting or not?"

Connor nods toward the round table in the middle of the break room, Kerrie puts out a bowl of jelly beans—her personal vice—and we settle down for our Thursday morning meeting where we review all current assignments and go over the budget.

Kerrie's in the process of giving us the bad news about how much our firewall upgrade is going to cost when an electric chime signals someone entering the reception area.

"And that's on the budget wish-list, too," Kerrie says, as she rises. "I'm the office manager, not the receptionist. We need to hire somebody, stat."

She disappears through the door, heading the short distance to the reception area. I can hear her speaking with someone, but can't make out words. Not that I'm really trying. We get a few walk-ins, but most clients come through referrals. Usually when someone walks in the front door it's because they're delivering a package or dropping off fliers for a new take-out restaurant.

So I'm not surprised when Kerrie returns quickly. But I am surprised by who I see with her.

Jezebel.

CHAPTER SIX

"RIGHT," Kerrie says, looking between me and Jez. "So, Connor? Could you and Cayden come with me to the file room? I'm having trouble, um, rebooting the server."

She heads out, and they both follow, but not before shooting me a half-dozen curious glances. I can't provide much insight, though. The fact is, I'm curious, too.

I gesture to the table. "Jelly bean?"

"Um, sure." She sits and pulls out a pink one.

"I guessed wrong," I say. "I would have pegged you for licorice."

She holds the candy between two fingers. "You think I'm not feminine enough for pink?"

"Not hardly," I say. I take the seat next to her, my knee brushing hers as I sit. "I just don't think it's you."

"Is that a fact?"

I reach for her hand, my fingers caressing her skin as I pluck the light pink bean out of her grip, then pop it into my mouth. "Sweet," I say, as her brows rise.

"And I'm not sweet?"

"I didn't say that."

She looks up at me, interested, as I pull a black bean from the bowl. "But you have a kick, too. Not to mention a classic pedigree." I put the candy in my mouth, and suck for a moment, noting with pleasure the way she squirms a little on the chair. And the way she doesn't meet my eyes. "And the truth is, I never think I'm going to enjoy the black ones, but each time I actually give them a whirl, I realize I can't get enough of them."

"Oh." She swallows, then licks her lips. "I always assumed they were an acquired taste."

"Nothing wrong with that, is there?"

She holds my gaze. "No. I suppose not."

"Maybe tonight I'll order you a glass of Sambuco. Like jelly beans with a buzz."

Her smile flickers, then dies.

"Okay, bourbon it is. Or wine." My quips don't reignite her smile, and I lean back in my chair. "All right, tell me the truth. Where did my banter go off the rails?"

I've obviously surprised her, and a laugh bubbles out. She presses her fingers over her lips and shakes her head. "Sorry. No, you're fine."

"Fine?" I study her. "Aren't you a lovely, little liar."

"No, really. I'm sorry, and you're banter's fine. I just mean that we won't be having that drink tonight."

The words are like a kick in the gut, but I hold it together. "Not a problem," I say. "We can jump straight to the sex."

She lifts a single brow, and for a moment I think it's arched in disapproval. But then I see the quick flicker of amusement in her eyes before she tilts her head and focuses on the jelly bean bowl.

She takes two of the mottled yellow ones. "These are

you. Popcorn jelly beans. Sweet and salty, and very unexpected."

I tilt my head. "That sounds remarkably like a compliment. But it can't be." I lean back in the chair, resting my head against my intertwined fingers. "Because if it were a compliment, you wouldn't be canceling our date. A date that I won, remember? I'm thinking we're facing a pretty serious rules violation here."

I mentally cringe. With such lame jokes, it's no wonder she's blowing me off. And although I'm tempted to give my groveling skills a run for their money, I'm not sure I'm ready to turn in my Man Card just yet.

"The compliment's coming," she says. "I'm cancelling our date because I want to hire you. To be Delilah's security detail, I mean. Well, not just you. Your whole shop as needed."

"Oh." I stand and go to the coffee maker, mostly because I don't want her to see the expression on my face. Honestly, I'm not entirely sure what she'd see on my face. Disappointment about tonight? Excitement about the job? Surprise that she'd offer? Especially considering she already had someone lined up...

"Why?" I ask, turning back to her. "I thought the studio had already arranged for someone?"

"Yeah, they had."

"And from your expression, I'm guessing that they're agreeing to the switch only because you took them off the hook for paying the bill."

"We're good for it, Mr. Blackwell. In case you were worried about the check bouncing."

"Never doubted it for a second. Coffee?" I grab a mug and hold it out for her. She shakes her head, and I put the mug back in the cabinet. "Larry," I say, and when I turn back to her, it's clear from her expression that my guess is dead-on. "This is about Larry."

Her shoulders rise and fall. "He trained you," she says, as if that's a full explanation. "And I don't know anything about the group that the studio hired."

"You don't know much about me, either."

"Like you said, I did some homework. And last night I saw you in action. And you're right."

"I usually am," I quip. "What am I right about now?"

"When you called my hotel room last night, remember? You said I trusted you." She tilts her chin, her eyes defiant. "You were right. I do. And so does Delilah."

I like the sound of those words more than I want to admit.

"And if I say that we don't have room on our docket? That we're serving our clients at capacity right now, and don't have the resources to take on someone new?"

She stands up and crosses to the counter, then leans back against it as she studies me cooly. "Is that something you're likely to say?"

I shouldn't, dammit. Hell, I shouldn't even be considering turning down this job, especially when just fifteen minutes ago I was standing in this room wishing that the job was mine, just so I could see her again.

And now here she is, offering me that very carrot. I should be ringing a damn Klaxon and letting Kerrie and the guys know we have a new client, and telling them we're about to celebrate by paying down some debt and balancing our ledgers.

I *should,* but now that she's here and I'm faced with the very reality I wished for, I can't quite conjure the enthusiasm, much less the words. Because this woman has gotten under my skin, and the temptation to have her in my bed is just too damn much. How the hell am I supposed to work side-by-side and not touch her?

And what if I do give in? What if I break all my rules and let myself succumb to this walking, talking temptation named Jezebel?

Either she'll slap my face—in which case I've fucked up our working relationship right there—or she'll melt in my arms.

Good in the moment, maybe. But I'm afraid that once she's in my bed, I won't want her to leave.

And that's the kind of complication I really don't need in my life.

"Pierce?"

"Yeah, right." I draw a breath. "Sorry, but we really are all booked up."

Her hips sway as she crosses to me in two long strides. She uses both hands to grab my collar, then levers herself close, her lips brushing my ear as she whispers, "Liar."

The words shoot straight through me, making my cock stiffen. And, yeah, forcing me to fight the urge to thrust my fingers in her hair, hold her head in place, and kiss her senseless.

Did I mention I find competence extremely sexy?

And she's either done her homework ... or she's an extremely good poker player.

Frankly, a woman who can bluff is pretty damn sexy, too.

She takes a few steps back, her mouth curved down into a frown. "Look, I know our first meeting was a little off the wall. I mean, I pretty much thought you were an incompetent ass."

"If you're trying to convince me to take the job, you're not doing a stellar job."

Her mouth twitches. "What I'm trying to say is that my perception has changed."

I take a step toward her, my eyes locked on hers. "So you don't think I'm an incompetent ass anymore?"

She's standing beside a chair, and her hand tightens on the back of it. But her eyes never leave my face. "You're still an ass," she says. Her voice has gone a little breathy. Just a little. Barely even something you'd notice if you weren't paying attention.

I was paying attention.

I take one more step closer. "But?"

She licks her lips, and damned if I don't crave that mouth. "But I think you're a competent ass."

"You're right. I am."

I'm standing in front of her, just inches away. I can smell her perfume, a subtle vanilla. I can feel her heat. I can see the way her blouse rises and falls with the quickening of her breath.

This is my chance.

I can slide my hand behind her neck and hold her still. I can crush my lips over hers and pull her body tight against mine. I can lose myself in the softness of her body, and feel my cock harden against her curves.

It would be so simple to pull her close. To claim her mouth, my tongue demanding and hard as we give in to one wild, ravenous kiss that leaves us both as breathless as sex.

I could do it all so easily.

I could ... but I don't.

Instead I slide my hands in my pockets. I turn away and face the table. And then I draw one deep breath.

"Pierce?"

"Let's go get a drink."

"A drink," she repeats, her voice flat. "I don't know if that's such a good—"

"It's almost five. I've had a long day. And we can talk about Delilah's schedule, your concerns, the job parameters. All that good stuff."

"So it's a business meeting." There's no intonation in her words at all. It's as if she's deliberately trying to strip them of any emotion. And as a result, I have no idea if she's relieved or disappointed.

"There's a bar a couple of blocks down. The Fix on Sixth. A friend owns it, so we should be able to score a table in the back, even during South By."

She's silent for a moment, obviously considering. Finally, she nods. "All right, then. Lead the way."

Kerrie's working on the computer in the reception area, and her brows rise as we enter the room from the hall.

"We'll be back in a few hours," I tell her. "Can you put together a standard client contract and leave it on my desk? Ms. Stuart can review it when we get back."

"Of course, sir." Her tone is entirely professional, but I know her well and can tell she's dying to ask me a thousand questions.

I open the door for Jez and guide her out into the elevator bank before Kerrie's overcome with curiosity, breaks protocol, and starts firing away.

We're waiting for the elevator when Jez says, "Your receptionist seems..."

"What?"

"Competent," she says, although it's obvious that wasn't her original thought.

I regard her curiously. "Really?" Kerrie *is* competent, but that isn't the vibe she's been projecting since Jez walked in. On the contrary, I'd say rampant curiosity was the emotion of the day.

"Actually, yes. But I was really going to say that she seemed curious." The elevator doors slide open, and she steps on, then glances back at me. "Is that because of me or you?"

"Both, I'm guessing. You, because of your sister. Me, because my sister's habit is sticking her nose into my business."

"Your sis—*oh*. So is this a family business?"

"Not in the way you mean," I say. "Kerrie started working for us when she got disillusioned with her last job. And as sisters go, she's not too much of a pain in the butt."

"You're older than she is."

"Ten years," I tell her. "She's twenty-four."

Jez nods. "I'm nine years older than Del. So there you go." She smiles up at me, and I'm struck by how much I like seeing her smile. "We both have younger sisters that we work with."

The elevator glides to a stop on the first floor, and I hold my hand over the door, ushering her out. "With that much in common, you may end up actually liking me."

She brushes my arm as she passes. "I like you," she says, and her soft words just about slay me. I want her. That's pretty much the bottom line. Because there's something about Jezebel Stuart. Something snarky. Something funny. Something sexy.

Sometimes even a little bitchy.

I don't know her well, but I've already seen that she's complicated and loyal, smart and committed.

She's a woman with layers, and so help me, I want to peel away each and every one of them.

And that's a dangerous way for a man like me to feel.

CHAPTER SEVEN

_____

"PIERCE?"

It's not her voice, but her hand gripping my elbow that pulls me from my thoughts.

We're outside now, standing at the southeast corner of Sixth and Congress, just outside my office building.

"Sorry. I was thinking." *About her.* "About security. Transportation. Everything."

"Glad to know you're on the ball. But which way?"

"Turn right," I say, pointing that direction. "We're just going a few blocks down."

Sixth Street is to Austin what Bourbon Street is to New Orleans. Only cleaner and classier and without the strip clubs. And usually without the drunk revelers vomiting in the street. During the SXSW festival, though, the distinctions between the two streets are minimal, and even this early, there are already packs of college students moving along the already crowded sidewalks.

The festival isn't limited to one location—in fact much of it takes place off Sixth Street at other venues and at performance tents set up along the river. But Austin hasn't dubbed itself the Live Music Capital of the World for nothing, and even when there's no festival in town, there's a lot of live music. Especially downtown.

The Fix is a few blocks from my office, an easy enough walk even in this crowd, and I expect it's going to be crowded since it's set up with a stage in the main room. Sure enough, I can see a band playing through the window, and there's a line of people, all wearing festival wristbands, waiting to get in.

"Maybe we should try somewhere else," she says, frowning at the line.

"Trust me." I take her hand to lead her toward the door, then feel a bit like a teenager when she doesn't pull away.

"Sorry," the door guy says. "We got a line. And you don't have a wristband."

"Tell Tyree it's Pierce Blackwell. We're not here for the music. I want to take the lady to the back."

The guy's young and skinny and pale—he's either a vampire or he's spent too many hours inside the university dorms—and he's making the most of his power over the door. He takes his time looking us up and down, then pulls a walkie-talkie out of the pocket of his jacket and signals for Tyree. For a moment, I consider that my friend might not be on site, in which case, I'll have to find someplace else to take Jez where we can get a seat despite the festival madness.

But then I see him approaching through the glass, a huge bear of a man whose beard and gold earring give him a pirate quality. Today, he's wearing a short sleeved black T-shirt with the Fix on Sixth logo, and the muscles under his dark cocoa skin flex as he reaches out to shake my hand.

"Haven't seen you in a week," he says, ushering me and Jez inside. "Where've you been?"

"Avoiding the crowds," I admit. "But I thought Jez

should see some of South By. And she can't visit Austin without getting her fix."

His teeth flash as he smiles. "Got that right. Nice to meet you, Jez," he says, his voice loud enough to hear over the R&B band. "I'm Tyree. Call me Ty. I own this dump."

"Hardly," she says, looking around. "It's great."

"It's got potential," he admits. To me he adds, "Renovations and repairs are kicking my ass. But I'll get it done."

"Ty and I served a tour together," I tell her. "Right before he traded in his uniform for a barman's apron."

"And a shit-ton of debt," he says. "This week we're in the black, though. So things are looking up. You here for the music?"

I shake my head. "Just the atmosphere. Jez and I need to talk. Thought I'd take her to the back."

"You know the way, my friend. Tell pretty boy back there I said to treat you well."

He's grinning, and I know he's talking about the new bartender, a grad student from the University whose name I can't remember.

"He's nice," Jez says. Her mouth is close to my ear, and I know that's only so she doesn't have to yell, but her proximity has the side effect of kicking my pulse up a notch. "I like him."

"Just don't cross him," I say, and she laughs.

"I'll remember."

We grab the only empty table and order two glasses of bourbon on the rocks. "So what do we need to talk about?" she asks, after the drinks come and she's taken her first sip. "Or did you just want to get me liquored up?"

"Would you think less of me if I said the latter?"

She hesitates only a second, then shakes her head. "No," she says, in the kind of low, sultry voice that runs over a man's skin like a ripple of fire. "But we both know it's a bad idea."

"You might be surprised how many bad ideas turn out to be very, very good."

Her smile fades, and she glances down at her drink, her finger tracing the rim.

"Jez?"

"Sorry." She looks up with a slow shake of her head. "It's just that we're here because of a bad idea that was just plain bad."

It takes me a second to parse the comment, but when I do, I say, "Levyl."

"Are you familiar with the whole story? Him and Delilah?"

"Yesterday I wasn't. Today, I have the basic Internet search version of the scandal."

"Scandal," she says, making the word sound as harsh as a curse. "A teenager should be able to make a few mistakes in her love life, but when hers blew up, it had to play out all over the tabloids and social media."

"Levyl's about her age, right?"

She nods. "He's a year older than Del. They started dating when she was seventeen. They did a movie together —he's the lead singer for Next Levyl."

"It's a boy band that won that TV show, right?"

"Exactly. And when the band hit, they were everywhere for a while, especially Levyl and the drummer. They got movies, TV shows, you name it."

"It wasn't on my radar," I admit. "But I vaguely remember hearing about him and the band."

"If you weren't dead, you heard about them. They were that popular. Still are, really, though it's settled into a more controlled insanity. But those first couple of years..." She trails off, shaking her head. "At any rate, Del and Levyl met when he was really exploding, and the world took a shine to them. Like the romance of the century. It was crazy—especially when she turned eighteen and the public started pressuring them to get engaged."

"Pressuring?"

"Fans on social media mostly," she explains. "But even talk show hosts would bring it up. It was crazy. And I think it was a little too much for Del. She adored Levyl—she still does—but when she went on location, and Garreth Todd was her co-star..."

I nod. "I read about that. Sounded to me like he seduced her."

"He did. Hell, he's admitted that much. And it didn't last—Garreth dumped her. But she's still the one who's vilified, because she broke Levyl's heart." Her voice is rising, and she takes a deep breath, obviously so that she can rein in her emotions. "Like I said, only eighteen and the whole world knows her private affairs."

"That's got to be horrible. I don't even like my sister nosing around in my life."

As I'd hoped, that makes her smile. "Yeah, well, that's the backstory. As for your part in all of this, you—"

"I think I got a sense of that last night."

"The crazed fans? Yeah, that's part of it. But the rest is all about my sister." I must look confused, because she goes on. "Levyl's coming here on Tuesday. I guess he's performing during the festival."

"And you think Delilah's going to want to see him?"

"Yeah. She's hurting. Those two together were combustible. Besides, it if was me, I would. If I'd hurt the man I loved? If I wanted to at least try to explain what happened and apologize? Yeah, I'd be all over that."

"They haven't talked since—"

"Just by phone. She cried for two days."

"Poor kid. What a mess." I rake my fingers through my hair, thinking. "We can get her to his concert. Get her safely backstage."

She shakes her head. "No, no you can't. Anything like that will leak. Right now, it's starting to die down—last night was nothing compared to what it's been. But if she goes there—if she sees him and it gets leaked—it's going to blow up again. She'll be vilified in the press again. Harassed on the set."

She signals for another drink, her expression harried. "Look, there can't be any scandal here, not even a hint of it. We can control her access to fans to keep it at a minimum, but if it blows up again—if what happened last night happens on a bigger scale—then my sister is pretty much out of a career."

I lean back, surprised by such a bold statement.

"I'm serious," she says, obviously seeing my confusion. "The studio's already fired her from one job—she was supposed to have a lead in a popular action franchise. And that would have been a huge payoff in terms of money and her clout in the industry. But when the scandal broke, they wouldn't touch her.

"But she has a contract," she continues, her words spilling out. "And so they put her in this. It's small and has next to no budget, but even so, they're just waiting for a reason to kick her off. And if the scandal kicks up again, they'll have their justification. I'm not supposed to know, but a friend who works in the executive offices told me. The lawyers have pretty much said that if the mess blows up, the producers can fire her and not be in breach of the contract."

"But she's in the middle of making the movie."

She shakes her head. "No. We've only just started. They could fire her and bring in someone else, easy."

I don't know what to say to that, and she must realize it, because she continues. "So that's what I need you for. That's the basic job parameters. You're protecting my sister from the fans, yeah. But mostly you're protecting her from herself. And if you fuck it up—if you lose her and she sneaks off to see Levyl or gets herself caught up in some sort of fan riot—I will fire your ass so fast it will make your head spin."

I study her, and it's easy to see that she's entirely serious. "And here I thought we were becoming friends."

"Competence impresses me, Mr. Blackwell. From what I've seen so far, you and your company fit the bill. Hopefully I won't be kicking my ass Wednesday morning."

"What's Wednesday?"

"The Austin part of the shoot is just a week. We fly from here back to Los Angeles. Everything else is on backlots and in the studio."

"I see." It's Thursday, and I'm more disappointed than I should be to know that she's leaving in just under a week.

"So that's pretty much it," she says, as the waitress delivers a fresh round of drinks. "Your typical teen celebrity security detail. Plus angst and scandal."

"I've got your back."

"Good," she says, lifting her drink. "Because if you fuck it up, I promise it won't be pretty."

I raise my drink as well, then hold it out to toast. As soon as she clinks her glass against mine, I take a sip, then put it back down, studying her.

"What?" she demands.

"You're not as tough as you pretend to be, Jezebel Stuart."

Her brow creases, and she glances down. I'd meant the words as a tease, but it's clear I've struck a nerve.

When she looks back up at me, there's a new kind of ferocity in her eyes. "I am," she says. "I didn't used to be— hell, I didn't want to be. But this job, this life…"

She trails off with a shrug. "Just don't fuck with me, okay?"

I want to reach across the table and take her hand. I want to pull her into my arms and hold her and tell her that I might not understand all the demons she's had to fight over the years, but that I will slay any that come near her now. I want to tell her that I'll keep her safe, whatever it takes.

But I know that this swell of emotion rushing up inside me is about the woman and not about the job, and so I push it back. Hold it in. And all I say is, "I wouldn't dream of it."

She swallows the rest of her drink and lets out a heavy sigh. "So I guess this job's not as sexy as what you usually do. Protecting state legislators or whatever."

"It's sexy enough." I take her glass from her hand and raise it to my lips.

"Oh," she says as she watches, her eyes on my mouth, as I take the last piece of ice. Then I reach for her hand. It's warm except for the chill on her fingers where she'd touched the glass, and I fight the urge to kiss those fingers to warm them.

She clears her throat, then tugs her hand from mine and puts it in her lap. "So, um, what else do you do?"

"A lot of basic protection, like you said. And since Austin's the capital, you're right about providing security to politicians. And we work with a lot of performers. Usually not with Del's Hollywood pedigree, but we've done security for some Grammy award winners who've performed at the Long Center and Bass Concert Hall."

"Any teen clients?"

"A few. One about a year ago stands out. I was still with my old firm then, but I took the job on my own, off book."

"What happened?"

I take a deep breath and think of Lisa. "Beautiful girl. Bubbly. Lots of fun. And very smart. Had a full ride at the University," I say, referring to the University of Texas, the prestigious, well-endowed institution that has helped shape Austin's culture.

"She was nineteen, and a stalker put his sights on her." It's a case I don't usually think about, and I take a long swallow, letting the bourbon burn down my throat, as the memories well up.

"What happened?"

"He attacked her—she was lucky. Got away with her life, but he slashed her face. Deep cuts with a jagged blade. And then he made clear that he intended to finish the job."

"She hired you?"

"She did. Well, her father did." Hire is a relative term. I met Lisa through Kerrie, who'd met her in Gregory Gym, where they both took a spin class. Since neither Lisa nor her dad had the money for the fee, I took the case as a barter, in exchange for her dad doing some custom cabinet work for my condo.

"What happened?"

"The stalker tried again." I start to raise the drink, then put it back down. "He's dead."

"You killed him."

I pause, then tilt my head in acknowledgement. To be honest, his death still haunts me. Not that I killed him—I'd do it again in a heartbeat—but what I saw in his eyes. I'd seen a lot of things during my time in the military, but I don't think I truly believed in evil until I looked at that man's face.

Jez is watching me, and I know she can feel the weight that's settled over our conversation. She says nothing, but she reaches out and takes my hand. My instinct is to pull away, but instead I hold on, surprised by how much the contact soothes.

But it only lasts a moment. Then, I gently pull away. "Sorry."

"No, it's—"

"I don't expect to be killing anyone on this job," I say, intentionally trying to add back some levity. "Unless of course the producer's an asshole. Then we can talk bonus."

A tentative smile touches her lips. "Fair enough." She tilts her head, looking at me. "So I guess you understand teenage clients. And it sounds like you're good with high maintenance clients from the entertainment world, too."

"Absolutely," I say, appreciating the tease in her voice. "But I have a feeling this assignment is going to be my favorite."

"Because of my sister?"

I meet her eyes, and the heaviness that had been in the air is finally brushed completely away, replaced by something equally dangerous. "No."

For a moment, we just look at each other, a faint pink rising in her cheeks. Then she finishes off her drink and reaches for the small wallet-style purse she'd left on the table. She slides the strap over her arm, then flashes an awkward smile. "We should probably go. I bet your sister has the contract ready."

"Sure." I stand, a little disappointed. I don't know why —it's not as if this were a date. As if we were going to leave the bar and head down Sixth Street, popping into various venues to drink and dance, her body pressed close to mine in the throng.

That wouldn't happen. But so long as we sit here, I can nurse the fantasy. And I hate that Jez has thrown reality back in my face.

She's three steps away from our table, and she looks back. "Coming?"

That's when I realize she's flustered, too. She hasn't given a thought to paying, and right now, she looks like a rabbit who's looking back at a hunter.

But this rabbit looks like she'd be happy to be devoured.

At least it's not just me.

I toss a hundred on the table—I happen to know the waitress, Melanie, is struggling to come up with the balance of her tuition—and follow Jez to the doorway into the main area.

The bar is coming to life, along with the street. And as in my fantasy, the crowd pushes us closer together. I take her hand, ostensibly to lead her to the door, but really because I just want to touch her, and by the time we reach the exit and step out into the cool night air, I'm breathing hard and sweat is beading on the back of my neck. Not from the exertion of getting out of there, but from the effort of fighting the urge to stay.

She's still holding my hand, and when I glance down and see our intertwined fingers, that's it. It's all over. I say a silent prayer and lift my head so that I can see her face, and there's so much heat reflected back that it almost melts me.

"Pierce," she says, but I just tug her toward me.

"Come on," I say, urging her down the street, faster than I should since she's wearing heels, but I can't wait. And when we've gone two blocks down the street, I pull her into the service alley by my office and press her against the wall, caging her in my arms.

"I'm sorry," I say. "But I have to." I thrust my fingers into that rich, dark hair, hold her head steady, and claim her mouth with mine.

It's probably the most wonderful, terrifying moment of my life. Jez, soft and warm in my arms, juxtaposed against the fear that she's going to shove me back and slap my face.

But she doesn't. Instead, her lips part more, and she leans into the kiss, her mouth as hot and wild as my own. She tastes of alcohol and desire, and my head swims, intoxicated by her surrender as much as by her touch.

One hand cups the back of my neck, pulling me closer. The other presses against my back, giving her leverage to arch up against me. Her hands are the most potent of aphrodisiacs, telling me without words that she wants this moment as much as I do, and my entire body tightens in response, need coiling through me. A wild craving. A desperate longing.

I'm hard as steel, and it's taking all my self-control not to slide my fingers through the slit of her skirt and tear the damn thing right off of her. I want to thrust my hands between her legs, then slip my fingers beneath the hot, wet silk of her panties. I crave the slippery heat of her desire on my fingertips. That sweet, slick evidence that proves how much she wants me.

I imagine bending my head and tasting her breasts. In my fantasies, I strip her bare and fuck her hard, our overheated bodies writhing together on cool, smooth sheets. My cock and fingers working a primal magic, sending her up and over and into the stars, until she explodes in my arms and begs me to do it again.

But I can't do that. Not really. And so this kiss—this

single, wild kiss in a filthy alley—is our stand-in for clean sheets and wild sex, and I thrust my tongue in deeper, making the most of it. She tastes like bourbon and sex, and as our tongues war and our teeth clash, I fear that this is so wild and so frantic that we're going to draw blood.

But I don't care. All I want is this moment. All I want is *her*.

She's practically melting against me, and I'm losing my mind. My thoughts reduced to basic, primitive needs, so powerful I can barely stand it.

My condo's only a few blocks away. I could step into the street. Grab a taxi, and take her home.

It would be a bold move. But then again, so was kissing her in an alley.

But, of course, we can't.

"Jez," I say, regretfully breaking the kiss. She opens her eyes, and by some miracle I grow even harder when I see the wild, blatant desire heating her eyes.

"We can't," she whispers, and though the words are like a knife, I know that they were inevitable.

"I know."

Her brow furrows. "Then why—?"

"Because I don't get involved with clients," I say, silently damning my own stringent rule. "But I had to taste you—just once—before we sign the contract."

CHAPTER EIGHT

ANYONE WHO'S EVER SAID that watching a movie being filmed is exciting is a goddamned liar. It's exciting for about the first fifteen minutes, when you've just arrived, and the crew is busy setting up lights or dressing the set or doing whatever it is that movie crews do.

Then you see how much sitting around it involves. Sitting and waiting and being quiet. And take after take after take.

I'm sure it's scintillating if you're in the cast or on the crew. But as an observer? Honestly, it's mind-numbing.

And yet here I am. Not because I think there's an immediate threat to Delilah—it's a closed set with its own security team—but because she's Blackwell-Lyon's responsibility, and this is my shift, and I need to understand her routine if I'm going to do my job.

So I'm sitting and watching and learning. I've seen three takes of Delilah's current scene, and while I don't know much about acting, I have to say I'm impressed with her skill. It's an angst-filled scene, and she's managed to kick me in the emotional balls all three times she's run through it.

But that's about as exciting as it gets, and since the entire scene is under four minutes and I've been sitting here for almost three hours, I'd say the return on investment is low.

"You do this every day?" I ask Jez, when she approaches my chair between takes. It's a director-style folding chair with a canvas seat and back. It doesn't, however, have my name on it.

"Exciting, isn't it?" she says dryly, and once again I'm struck by how much I like this woman. We're simpatico, she and I.

"As much fun as watching grass grow."

"Watching action scenes is fun, though," she tells me. "When the stunt double comes in, especially."

"Now you're talking," I say, willing to hold out for this tiny thrill. "When are they shooting that?"

"They're not." A hint of a smile flashes. "That was in the movie she got fired from. This one's all deep emotion and torment." She pats me on the shoulder. "Enjoy."

"Where are you off to now?"

"Back to the hotel. I can't get a decent signal here, and I have a video call scheduled with Delilah's agent, then her publicist, and then her accountant. I'll be lucky if I survive the day without my head exploding. You're good?"

I want to tell her I'd be better if she stayed. I've barely seen her since we arrived, and while I'm here to work, the truth is I missed her last night.

After we got back to my office and finished the paperwork, I'd planned to go back to the hotel with her. But Jez shut me down. "Del's already tucked away in her room and the floor is secure, right?"

"Right," I admitted. And that was all well and good, but I knew the real reason was that she wanted time away to clear her head. And as much as I regretted the distance, I had to admit that was probably smart.

"Fine," I say now. "Del and I will see you at the hotel after the shoot."

She heads out, and since the cast and crew are pulling long days, I settle in for another nine hours of soul-crushing non-excitement.

Fortunately, I only have to wait an hour before Delilah comes by and flops on the ground beside my chair. "I am *so* wiped out," she says. "But I have forty-five minutes until we start up again." She passes me a wrapped sandwich. "Want? The powers that be are making me eat salad."

From the tone of her voice, you'd think they were making her eat gruel.

She's wearing skinny jeans and a *Keep Austin Weird* T-shirt. Her damp hair is pulled back into a ponytail, and she's wearing no make-up. I assume she showered in her trailer before heading my way. Presumably, there's another hair and make-up session scheduled for after lunch.

All in all, she looks like she could be a freshman at UT, and she's at least as laid back as any local Austin girl. She crosses her legs then peels open the lid from her salad. "I'm ravenous. Tonight, when we get back to the hotel, I'm going to actually eat." She looks at me. "How about you? Gonna stay for room service? I'm thinking we need to order all the fries. Like, *all* the fries."

"No salad and quinoa for you tonight?"

She wrinkles her nose. "Don't rat me out, okay? I'll have a hard enough time when I get back to LA and my trainer kicks my ass. But while I'm here, I'm eating when I can. Besides, I'm fully clothed in this movie. No love scenes. No showers. No slow-mo shots of me in a bikini running on a beach. Honestly, it's nice to just act, you know?"

"Not really," I admit. "But I'll take your word for it."

Del smiles, and that's when I can really see her star power. It's bright and photogenic and lights up the set.

"You like her, don't you?"

"Who?" I ask, though I know perfectly well who she's talking about. And like Pavlov's dog, my pulse has sped up just at the mention of Jez.

"My sister. She's not really a bitch, you know."

"Sure she is," I quip, making Del laugh.

"Okay, fine. Maybe she is. But you like her anyway."

"Yeah," I admit. "I do."

"Good." She sounds smug. "And just so you know, Jez has reasons."

"I don't think she's a bitch," I say, though I don't mention that I've definitely witnessed some bitchy moments. "But what are the reasons?"

"That stupid book, of course."

I frown. "What stupid book?"

"That tell-all book that my old bodyguard wrote."

"Larry?" That can't be true.

"Oh, no. The guy who came after. Simpson. The prick. He called the book *The Stuarts of Beverly Hills*. It was total trash—one of those things they published superfast to get in on all the drama with me and Levyl and Garreth—but he said some pretty shitty things about Jezebel in it, too."

She lifts her shoulder. "They got pretty close, if you know what I mean. So now she's careful. That's why we've only had a series of rent-a-guards since she fired him. But it's hard not really knowing the guys who are watching over you, you know?" Her words are flying fast, and I wonder if it's because as an actress she's usually scripted, so she's taking advantage of being off book.

"At any rate," she continues, before I can get a word in,

"sometimes she comes off as bitchy, but it's only because she's protecting us."

I'm gripping the wooden arms of the chair so tight I'm probably leaving dents. And I swear if this asshole Simpson was on the set right now, he'd be a dead man.

"Anyway," she says, standing up and brushing the dust off her jeans. "I just thought you should know. In case she seems, you know, distant."

"I'm just working for her, Del. There's nothing going on."

"Of course not," she says, but right then I doubt her acting skills, because she really doesn't sound convincing.

As soon as she heads off to the trailer to get in make-up for her next scene, I pull out my phone, open a web browser, find a digital copy of the book, and settle in to read.

Immediately, my blood starts to boil. He talks about how their parents died, and how Jez stepped in as head of the family and manager of Del's career, which was already on track, as the girl had been discovered at age six. He gives details about Del's dating and how she met Levyl and her interactions with fans. He runs though arguments between Jez and Del. Reveals their conversations, their habits, the details of their lives.

It's not skanky, but it's invasive as shit. He's told the world things that only someone close and with access would know.

In other words, he broke their trust.

Bastard.

I finish the book about an hour before Del wraps for the day, which is good, because that gives me a chance to quit seething before we get into the Range Rover and head for the Starfire.

"I ordered some food," Jez says when we arrive at the

suite. She points to the spread laid out on the suite's dining room table, and Del squeals and claps her hands.

"These are for me," Del says, taking the entire basket of fries. "I'm going to go gorge myself in my room and watch bad reality television." She flashes me a mischievous smile, and I can't help but think that she's leaving us alone on purpose. And not so that we can talk business.

"Hey," I say, after Del's gone. "How was your day?"

Jez presses her fingers to her temples. "Crazy."

"Bad crazy?"

"No," she says, "just busy crazy." She glances at the table. "We're going to talk shop, so does that mean you're still on duty?"

"If you're asking if I can have some of that wine, I think I can go for it."

"Good. Because I don't want to drink alone, and I need one." She passes me the bottle and a corkscrew. "I didn't think to have the waiter open it. You'll do the honors?"

I take the bottle, and open the wine, then pour us each a glass. "Cayden texted me as we were pulling in. He's gone over security with the staff, and the other two guests on this floor checked out this morning. Blackwell-Lyon now holds those rooms through Thursday." Which means no one outside of our team and the hotel staff can access this floor. And as far as security goes, that's a very good thing.

"Really? That's going above and beyond."

"Nothing's beyond if it keeps you safe. And Cayden's one hell of a negotiator. You won't find a surprise charge for those rooms on your bill—from us or from the hotel."

"If paying for those rooms keeps Del out of the middle of the kind of melee you saw the other night, I'd happily pay for them."

"I know." I take a seat on the sofa, then indicate the

cushion next to me. "You've proven over and over again how much you're willing to sacrifice for your sister."

"I have," she says, sitting beside me without hesitation. She's wearing a white V-neck T-shirt and a gray skirt made out of some sort of stretchy material. Her feet are bare, and I get the feeling this is Jezebel's typical work-at-home uniform. Still professional, but not as buttoned up as the pantsuit she'd been wearing on set this morning.

"Not that I think of any of it as a sacrifice," she continues. "It's just—"

She cuts herself off sharply, then turns to look at me, frowning. "I've *proven over and over again*. That's what you said."

"Yeah."

For a moment, she's silent, her brow furrowed as if she were trying to solve a knotty math problem. Then it clears, and she says, "*Fuck,*" so softly I almost don't hear her. She puts her glass on the table, then stands, then turns to look at me.

"You read the book." The words are an accusation, and she doesn't specify *what* book. Clearly, she knows she doesn't need to. "Del shouldn't have told you about that," she says, not waiting for me to answer.

"I read it today," I admit. "And I think Del was trying to help."

"Help?" Her brows rise. "Help how?"

"Help me," I clarify. "She realized that I want to get to know you better."

"Great. Just great. Because that book's certainly the way to do that. *Fuck,*" she repeats, and this time I hear her just fine.

"He was an ass," I say. She's turned away from me, and

now I gently take her elbow and urge her back to face me. "Simpson was an ass who broke your trust."

"Isn't that the truth?" She thrusts her fingers in her hair, lifting it up before letting it fall back in waves around her face. I know the gesture came out of frustration, but the look is sexy as hell, and it's all I can do not to gather her close.

"Do you want to talk about it?"

She shrugs, then goes over to the table and plucks a tortilla chip out of a ceramic bowl. She dips it in salsa, then takes a bite. I assume that's her way of saying no, so I'm surprised when she carries the chips and salsa to the couch and puts them on the coffee table. She sits again, this time tucking one foot under her so that she's facing me.

"I didn't have my guard up," she says. "I'd gotten so used to trusting someone, that I just let down all my walls."

"Larry," I say, and she nods.

"He was like a dad to me. It was easy, you know? And then he retired and moved to Orange County, and I hired Simpson. And I guess I was primed to trust." She licks her lips, then takes a sip of wine. "I let him get too close."

I nod. I'd guessed as much.

"And then when the book came out—" Her voice breaks, and I take her hand. I'm not sure if I should, but right now, I need to touch her, not just for her, but for me. "I wanted to go cry to Larry, but the accident—he was already dead. And—" Her voice breaks, and she visibly gathers herself. "And I thought, *well, at least he can't see my humiliation.*"

"Jez..."

"I complained to him. Simpson, I mean." She laughs harshly. "Isn't that a nice way of putting it? I lost my shit. I ranted and screamed and I think I threw a book at him." She closes her eyes and takes a deep breath. I squeeze her hand, and when she squeezes back, she looks at me gratefully.

"He flat out told me that since everything in the book was true, I couldn't do a thing about it. And then—" Her breath hitches. "And then he said that I was lucky he didn't talk about how lousy I was in bed."

She makes a noise like a gasp and leaps to her feet, her hand going over her mouth. I stand behind her, my hands on her shoulders. "If I ever meet him, I swear I'll put him in the ground. He doesn't deserve to breathe the same air as you."

Her shoulders start to shake, and I gently turn her so that she can press her face against my chest and cry while I hold her.

"I'm sorry," she says after a while, as she pulls away. "And oh, man, I got your shirt all wet."

"It'll dry."

She flashes a watery smile. "You're—unexpected."

"Am I?" I turn the word over in my head. "In a good way or a bad way?"

"Good." She brushes a finger under her eyes, drying her tears. Then she nods, as if reassuring herself. "Yeah, good. Although why the hell I'm telling you any of this, I don't know."

"Because I brought it up," I suggest. "Because you need someone to talk to. Because Simpson's bullshit was part of the price you pay for celebrity, and so was that mess we ran into at the Crown the other night."

"All true," she says. "And all so goddamned unfair."

I take her hand and urge her back to the sofa. "Stretch out," I say, and when she does, I put her feet in my lap. Her toes are painted a pale pink, and she looks like she hasn't gone a day without a pedicure. And when I rub my thumb along her arch, she tilts her head back and moans.

I want to hear that moan again—and not because of a foot massage.

"Why unfair?" I ask. "I mean, other than the obvious."

"Nothing. I shouldn't even—Hey," she snaps when I take my hands off her feet.

"Truth," I say. "Or no massage for you."

She scowls at me, but nods. Then she tilts her head back and closes her eyes. "You read the book, so you know what happened. Our parents died in an accident, and instead of starting college, I stepped in as Del's manager. I didn't trust anyone else, and my mom had been doing it for years, so I sort of knew the ropes. And I knew Mom would want me to. Plus, I love my sister. I do."

"But?"

"But I never had the chance to figure out what I want to do. And all I know is that I don't like this life. I don't like living in LA. I don't like being in the spotlight."

She opens her eyes and shrugs. "So that's it. That's my guilty secret."

"Why don't you stop?"

"I will, but not until Del's ready. In a lot of ways she's mature, but she's also been incredibly sheltered. Leaving her now would be a recipe for disaster."

"She might surprise you."

"She might. But that's not a risk I want to take. She's too important to me."

"So you have a plan," I say, taking my hand from her foot and moving to massage her calves.

"That feels amazing—you're *so* hired. And yes, I have a plan. And until then, I'll just suck it up and live with the drama."

"You can manage." I'm barely paying attention to my words. Instead, I'm sinking fast into the feel of her. The smoothness of her skin. The heat of her body.

"And it's crazy," she continues, "because as much as I hate it is how much Del loves it. She thrives on this life. Even the scandal doesn't bother her. She just wants to act."

"What about you? What do you want?"

She sits up, then pulls her legs back and tucks them under her, as if the question has made her uncomfortable. "I honestly don't know."

Her voice is soft, barely a whisper. But I hear the truth in her words, and I want to pull her into my arms and hold her close.

"No? Not even a little thing?" I tease. "Dark chocolate with sea salt? More tortilla chips? World peace?"

"Honestly, right now I just want—"

"What?"

She sighs. "I just want to take a shower and crawl into bed. It's been a long day."

Her words shred me. I didn't realize how much I wanted to stay until she yanked the possibility out from under me. "Sure," I say. "Of course."

I rise. "I'll let you rest. Tomorrow's a night shoot, right? I'll call you in the morning and we can talk time and logistics. In the meantime," I add as I head for the door, "you know the protocol. Don't leave this floor without coming to get me. "I'm going to crash in the room on the end."

"Pierce?"

I hesitate, my hand on the knob. "Yeah?"

"I lied."

I turn, something in the tone of her voice firing my senses and making my cock grow hard. "Did you?"

She stands up, then takes a step toward me. "I don't want to sleep."

I take a corresponding step toward her. "No? Then what do you want?"

I hear the tremor in her breath. Then I watch as she comes one step closer. Then another and another, until she's just inches away from me. She meets my eyes, and her gaze never wavers. "I want you to kiss me," she says.

Her words ignite inside me, and I have to shove my hands into my pockets to keep from yanking her into my arms. And it just about kills me to say what I have to. "I told you. I don't sleep with clients. And you don't sleep with anyone on your payroll, remember?"

"I'm not asking you to." She comes closer, and I can smell her vanilla scent. And that's not good, because right then, I want to devour her. "I just want a kiss."

"Jez..."

"Here," she says, pressing her index finger to the corner of her mouth. "Just one little kiss."

Her eyes are locked on mine, and right then I'd swear she had super powers, because I have no will to fight. I can only lean in, my lips brushing softly over the corner of her mouth.

"Good?" I ask.

"Yes," she says, but she's shaking her head no. And her eyes tell me that she wants more.

I lean back, my pulse pounding as I look at her. Her parted lips. Her heavy lids. Her tousled hair.

Her chest rises and falls with each breath, and I'm certain that she's as turned on as I am. She swallows, and I watch the way her throat moves, fighting the urge to lean in and kiss that little indentation at the base of her neck.

I let my gaze dip lower, taking in the curve of her breasts

and her nipples, hard beneath the thin material of her bra and T-shirt. It's hemmed at the waist and not tucked in, and I know that if I were to reach out, I could press my hand against her abdomen and feel her muscles tremble as she sucks in a breath.

And if I went lower...

Well, I can't help but wonder what she's wearing under that skirt. A thong, I imagine, or nothing at all, because the material clings smoothly to her hips and legs. And if I slip my hand between her thighs, would I find her already wet?

I think I would, and the thought makes me hard.

I should walk away—I know that. But when you get right down to it, I've never been one to follow the rules. And sometimes, doing the right thing is highly overrated.

"Jez," I whisper, and then I don't even give her time to respond. Because, dammit, I can't risk her saying no. So I swoop down, claiming her mouth, holding her close. She tastes like wine and sin, and I want to get drunk on both. Intoxicated by her touch. Her taste.

"Kisses," I murmur, holding her chin as I look deep in her eyes. "That's what you want? Like this?" I ask, brushing my lips over hers. "Or like this?" I demand, trailing a line of kisses down her neck to the soft indentation at her collarbone.

She trembles under my touch, and the only sound she makes is a soft, breathy, "Yes."

"Jez," I murmur, but her name is muffled by my mouth on her breast, over her bra and shirt. She arches back, her shoulders resting on the wall behind her, the angle of her body now giving me better access. But I want to taste her, not the shirt, and I slide my hands up, taking the shirt with me, until I've exposed her white, cotton bra.

It's unlined, and her nipples are like pebbles against the

thin material. I close my mouth over one breast and suck, then use my teeth to tease her nipple. She cries out, then whimpers when I pull back, releasing her.

But I'm not letting her off that easily. On the contrary, I'm still on my quest for skin, and I use my teeth to pluck up the edge of the bra and yank it down, freeing her breast.

She's gasping, her fingers sliding into my hair as she presses me closer, forcing my mouth where she wants it, and I use my tongue to tease her nipple until I feel her start to tremble and I know that there is no way—no way—that I am going to let her come without tasting her sweet pussy.

She whimpers when I pull away, then blow a stream of air on her now-wet breast. "Please," she begs as I brush a line of kisses right at her bra line. "Pierce, please."

"Shhh." I lift my mouth from her skin long enough for a single command. "Not a word," I order as I slide my hands down to the waistband of her skirt. It's a pull-on style, but I don't push it down over her hips. Instead, I inch the material up—higher and higher until the skirt barely covers her, and I press my hand against her inner thigh and slowly stroke my way up.

She's trembling, and her soft noises are making me crazy, and I'm so fucking hard it's painful. But right now, all I care about is touching her. I want to feel her, hot and slick on my fingers, and I'm so, so close.

Mostly, I want to taste her. To flick my tongue over her clit. To suck and kiss and tease until she explodes against my mouth.

Just a kiss, just like we said.

But it's the most intimate kiss of all.

Slowly, my fingers rise. She's wearing a barely-there thong, and I impatiently yank it down, uncovering her slick heat. And at the same time, I keep my kisses coming, lower and lower, until there's no more skirt, just flesh, just *her*, and she's waxed and smooth and wonderful.

"Please," she begs as I close my mouth over her. As my tongue finds her clit. As my fingers thrust inside her in time with my intimate kisses, my tongue laving her. My lips tormenting her.

Her hips start to move, and she's riding my mouth, her hands in my hair guiding me. And I'm getting harder and harder as I hear her raw, passionate noises. And all I want to do is make her come. Make her explode.

And know that I'm the man who took her over the edge.

"Yes!" she cries, and her body trembles, her pussy clenching tight around my fingers.

I'm already on my knees, but now her legs give out, and she tumbles to the ground, pulling me down with her.

My hands are all over her. Touching her. Stroking her. Listening to her soft sounds, her needy murmurs. "I can't get enough of you." And it's true. I've tasted her—now I want to claim her. Hard and hot and fast, then softly. Tenderly. I want to feel her break into a million pieces, and I want to be deep inside her, her body tight around my cock, when I come.

"Good," she says. "Because I want more, too." Her face is buried against my chest, but now she rises, her face and torso lifting as she meets my eyes. "I want so much more."

She unbuttons my shirt, then brushes a kiss on my breastbone. She starts to kiss her way down, lower and lower until my already stiff cock is so hard against my jeans it's almost painful. Her hand cups me through the denim, and I arch back, trying to steady my breathing. And when her fingers unbutton my fly, it's a goddamned miracle that I don't come right then.

She shifts her position, and I know she's about to pull

out my cock and take me in that hot little mouth, which sounds like a slice of heaven. Except it's not enough. Dammit all, it's just not enough.

I reach down and cup her face. Her eyes flicker in confusion. "*More*," I say.

She licks her lips, looking so damn tempted. "We both have rules."

"I think we've bent those rules so much, they're twistier than nautical knots."

Her teeth drag over her lower lip, and I chuckle.

"A woman with integrity," I say. "I can't fault that."

"Pierce?"

"Hmmm?"

"You're fired."

CHAPTER NINE

YOU'RE FIRED.

I don't think I've ever heard such magical words.

The kind of words that set me free. That open up all sorts of wonderful, decadent, intimate possibilities.

The kind of words that fire my blood and make me hard.

The sound of her voice has barely faded when I have her arms above her head, her wrists crossed, and my hand holding her in place. Her T-shirt is still awry, her bra all twisted up. Her skirt is around her waist, and her panties are around one ankle.

She looks wild and ready and absolutely beautiful.

"I'm a free agent now," I say. "Imagine the possibilities."

"I want to do more than imagine," she says. "I want to be so sore I can barely walk tomorrow. I want—"

"What?"

"I want tonight. I'll hire you again in the morning, but dammit, Pierce, right now, I want you inside me."

I'm still mostly dressed, too, but I don't care, and from

the way she's begging me, neither does she. "Now," she demands. "Pierce, please. Now."

I release her wrists so I can unbutton my fly, and it's only then that I realize I don't have a condom. Which is ironic, since I *always* use a condom.

"I don't either," she says when I tell her as much. "But I'm clean, and I'm on birth control."

"I've been tested," I tell her. "I'm safe. Do you trust me?"

I watch her eyes as she answers, and damned if her soft, sincere "yes" isn't the most erotic sound ever.

"Good," I say, "because I can't wait."

"Me neither." She reaches for me, pulling me on top of her and claiming my mouth with the kind of intensity that makes a kiss feel like a fuck.

"Baby," I say. "I don't think I can go slow."

"Don't," she begs. "Don't you dare go slow."

I meant what I said. I couldn't go slow if I tried. I've wanted her since I first saw her at Thyme, and now that she's half-naked and beneath me, I can't hold back. Not the first time, anyway.

I ease my hand between her legs, stroking her. Opening her.

She arches up, meeting my movements, body lithe and warm and ready.

She's slick and beautiful, and I ease over her, then tease her pussy with the head of my cock, just to make us both a little more crazed.

But Jez is having none of it, and she reaches down, her hand closing around my shaft as she guides me to her center. "Now," she demands. "Dammit, Pierce, I want you inside me," and her words are so hot and desperate that I can't hold back. Can't even take it easy. And I thrust inside her. Once, twice. Deeper each time, until I'm so deep and tight that it seems like I'm going to lose myself.

I piston inside her, my weight on my hands against the floor, her hips rising up to meet me. And her eyes—her eyes are locked on mine.

I'm close, so damn close, but I'm not ready to come yet. "Over," I say on a gasp. "Get on top."

With my hands on her waist, I roll us over, and it's so fucking sexy watching her ride my cock that I still may not last.

"Clothes off," I order, flicking my eyes over her clothes as I reach between our bodies and tease her clit with my fingertip. "There you go," I say, as her core clenches around me, tightening with her coming explosion.

She rips her shirt and bra off, then yanks the skirt over her head as well. She's fully naked now, and I'm still completely dressed except for my open fly, and it's so damn sexy that I know I'm going to lose it soon. "Come on," I urge her. "Come with me."

"Yes," she says as I stroke her. "Oh, God, yes, don't stop."

But I wouldn't dream of stopping, and I play with her pussy as she rides me—and then, as she cries out that she's coming, and she clenches tight around my cock—I empty myself inside her, the orgasm rolling over me with the force of a goddamned tidal wave.

And then, when I'm spent, she collapses on top of me, her breasts against my shirt, her lips brushing just above my collar.

I take her chin and guide her mouth to mine, then kiss her long and deep. "Baby," I say, when we come up for air, "you feel like heaven."

"Funny. I thought that was you."

I chuckle, then slide out from under her. "Come here," I say, as I pick her up. She curls against me, naked and soft, and I carry her to the bedroom, only then realizing how lucky we were that Del didn't decide to leave her bedroom to go get a snack.

I put Jez in bed, then strip and slide in next to her. She's wiped me out, but unlike my usual encounters, I'm not inclined to leave. On the contrary, I want to stay. I want to spoon against her. Which, right there, tells me something about the way I feel about this woman. Because I'm not a guy who spoons.

Except with Jezebel, apparently I am.

She's warm and her ass is nestled against my crotch, and despite the fact that I'm both spent and exhausted, I want her again.

I can wait, though. It feels too good just holding her.

I know I should move. Should get up and go to my own room. Make a cup of coffee. Do something.

But I can't quite manage, and the longer I stay like this the deeper I slide down toward sleep.

"Pierce?"

The sound of my name pulls me back with a jolt. "Sorry, sorry. I didn't mean to doze off." I sit up, groggy and confused, and kicking myself for not having gotten out of here sooner.

"I'll get out of your hair," I say, as I push myself upright and sit on the edge of the bed, my back to her as I try to locate my clothes in the dark.

"No, no, wait."

Something in her tone worries me, but when I twist around to face her, I can't read her expression. "Jezebel? Baby, what is it?"

"You're not—you're not dating anyone, right? I'm not being the other woman?"

I almost laugh. I'm about as far away from attached as a man can get. And at least until I met Jez, that was fine by me. Now—well, I'm not exactly looking to pop the question, but I can't deny that she's made me reconsider my one-night-then-move-on *modus operandi*. Because I could definitely handle two nights with this woman. Frankly, three would be just fine, too.

"Pierce?" There's worry in her eyes, and I realize my hesitation made her doubt.

"I'm not," I say hurriedly. "Not by a long shot."

"Oh." The relief in her voice is palpable. "Good. I mean, I'd assumed you were single. Because you'd said you were meeting a blind date that night we met. I'm guessing Kerrie set you up."

"Not exactly." The words spill out automatically, and I immediately wonder what the fuck I'm doing. Just say *yes*. Just agree and be done with it, because what does it matter?

"Not exactly a blind date? Or not exactly Kerrie?"

"It wasn't a blind date. And Kerrie had nothing to do with it." *Idiot.* I'm an idiot who has no control over the words that come out of his mouth.

Except I'm not. Not really. Because for better or for worse, I don't want to pull my punches with this woman. This is new territory for me—but there's no denying the way I feel.

"Not a blind date," she muses. "But you didn't know what she looked like and—*Oh!* The initials. I read about that somewhere. That new app." She grins at me, and thankfully she looks amused and not scandalized. "You had me confused with a hook-up."

"Which was a horrible mistake," I say, then lean in to

brush a kiss over her lips. "Because you are so much more than that."

Once again, I hear my words and can't believe I'm saying them.

At the same time, I can't deny that they're true.

Del had it wrong—Jez isn't a bitch, she's a witch. And somehow, she's completely enchanted me.

"So why no girlfriend?" she asks.

"Complaining?"

"Hardly. I'm curious." She shifts to sit up in bed, pulling the sheet up to cover her breasts, which seems a damn shame to me.

I lie down again, my arm up over my head. I consider ignoring the question. Changing the subject or, better yet, distracting her by pulling her on top of me and taking her again, hard and fast.

But there's the problem of that spell she's cast. I want to talk to her. I actually want to stay here in bed with her and have a conversation about my past. Seriously, it's the damnedest thing.

"So?" she presses. "Are you about to tell me to mind my own business?"

"No," I say, and manage to bite my tongue before I say that I'd like to make it her business. "Just gathering my thoughts."

She clicks on the bedside lamp, then slides out of bed, and I enjoy the view of her naked back disappearing into the living room. Then I enjoy even more the full frontal view when she returns with two glasses of wine.

"Just fyi," I say. "Wandering around naked tends to not be conducive to talking. For future reference."

She hands me a glass as I prop myself up in bed, then puts hers on a side table. She slides back in and wraps the sheet around her. "Noted. You were saying? About your pathetic lack of a girlfriend or wife?"

I shake my head, amused, then take a sip of wine, still not sure how to begin. Finally, I cut to the chase, "I survived the military," I say. "I didn't survive my engagement."

"What happened?"

"I loved her. I thought she loved me. And then three hours before the wedding she told me that she couldn't go through with it. That she didn't love me. That she wasn't sure she ever had."

She presses her hand over mine. "That bitch. Oh, Pierce. I'm so sorry."

"I'm over it." I shrug like it was no big deal, even though of course it meant everything. I meet her eyes. "But I don't do relationships."

Her brows rise. "You're looking at me as if that's an issue. It's not."

"Right," I say, and though that's exactly what I should want to hear, the words still hit me hard before sitting in my stomach like a ball of lead.

"I'm only here for a few more days, remember? And until Del is ready to run her own career, my focus is on her, not relationships, not dating, not any of it."

The hint of a smile blooms wide as she gestures between us. "I don't regret this at all, but I'm not a shrinking violet of a girl who's been suddenly mesmerized by your magical, mystical cock."

"It is pretty spectacular, isn't it?"

"I'm not about to say anything to add to that ego," she says. "What about these women on the app? Aren't they looking for relationships?"

"It's not that kind of app. Plus, I make it clear. I'm just in it for the night."

"Really? How mercenary."

"It's worked for me so far." But even as I say it, I can't shake the feeling that my brick wall of one-night stands is about to come crashing down.

"Hmm."

"You don't approve."

"On the contrary, it's pretty smart." She lies back down, then props herself up on her elbow. "Maybe I should follow your lead."

I frown, not understanding. "What are you talking about?"

She stretches out, her head now on the pillow so that she's facing the ceiling. "It's just a good way not to be alone, right?"

"Sure," I say automatically. But that's a lie. I'm always alone with those women. And as much as I hate admitting it, being here with Jez—touching her, talking to her—has only driven that simple fact home.

For a moment, we're both quiet. Then she sits up again and pulls her knees to her chest and wraps her arms around them. "We're getting far too maudlin. So here's what I was thinking. About tomorrow, I mean. Del and I are scheduled for a full day at the spa, and then at seven she has to be on the set for the night shots."

"Right," I say, more disappointed than I should be that I won't be seeing her during the day. "And I'll be here at six to pick you two up."

"Well, yeah. I mean, unless you have time during the day."

"Of course I do. This is a full-time gig, remember? But if you're suggesting I get a pedicure, I think I'll pass. But Connor's scheduled to be with Del tomorrow until five. Maybe he'd like a facial."

"Very funny. No, it's just that I was thinking."

"About?"

"Del. And how she might have more fun doing a spa day with someone closer to her own age."

"Uh-huh."

"Right," she says, then clears her throat. "You told me Kerrie's twenty-four, right?"

"Kerrie? Yeah."

"That's close. Do you think she'd be up for it?"

"A spa day with a movie star who also has a wicked sense of humor? Yeah, I think she'd be on board." I do my best not to anticipate where else this is going. But I'm seeing a long, lazy day stretched out in bed with Jez, while Connor watches over the girls at the spa.

"And I was thinking that maybe you and I could—"

"Yes."

"—do Austin," she finishes.

I sit up. "Wait. What?"

She frowns. "What did you think I was going to say?"

"Nothing. Backgammon. Something like that."

Her laugh fills the room like music. "Well, I think *backgammon* can be on the menu. But I've only been to Austin once before, and I was hoping you could show me around."

That sounds remarkably like a date to me. And while I would be enthusiastically on board with spending the entire day naked and in bed, the idea of a date causes a chorus of *Danger, Will Robinson* to ring in my head.

Because I don't do relationships. I don't.

But somehow when I'm around Jez, I have to keep reminding myself of that.

Then again, she's already pointed out that she's leaving in less than a week. And I have no real indication that she's reading anything more into spending the day together than simply spending the day together.

Which I want to do.

More than I probably should, actually.

"Pierce?" She's frowning at me. "I didn't think it was that hard a question. Are you—"

"I'm in," I say, because I'll be damned if I'm going to let someone else show her around town. "Just thinking about where we'll go."

"Great. Good." She breathes deep, then yawns.

I slide out of bed and scan the room, looking for my pants. "I'll let you sleep. I'll go text Kerrie and Connor, and then tomorrow after we get them settled at the spa, you and I will hit the town."

"Okay," she says, but I can hear the hesitation.

"Problem?"

"It's just that at six o'clock tomorrow I have to hire you again. I was thinking that so long as you're not on payroll right now..."

"Are you asking me to sleep here, Ms. Stuart?"

She sits up, letting the sheet fall away. "Actually, Mr. Blackwell. I'm not asking you to sleep at all."

CHAPTER TEN

"THIS PLACE IS AWESOME," Jez says to me, glancing up at the toy pterodactyl hanging from the ceiling. "And these pancakes are amazing. I've never had gingerbread before."

"Never?"

"I've led a sheltered life," she says, her voice totally deadpan.

I laugh and hold my cup up for a coffee refill as our waiter passes by. We're on South Congress at Magnolia Cafe, my favorite restaurant in Austin, second only to the original Magnolia Cafe on the other side of the river. It has a laid-back atmosphere, tons of character, and food that I'm willing to go out of my way for.

In this case, it's not out of the way at all. Not only are we just a couple of miles from the Starfire Hotel, but we're also right at the south end of the SoCo shopping area. And since Jez told me that she wanted to buy a souvenir for Del today, I figured we'd spend some time window-shopping our way back toward the river.

"We're lucky we got in," I say. "This place is usually

jam-packed on Saturdays, especially during South By." I glance around—it's crowded, but not crazy busy.

"It's not yet ten," she says. "Anyone who was out late last night is probably still asleep." Her teeth graze her lower lip as she looks up at me through her lashes. "I know I'd still be asleep after my very late night if it weren't for having to get my sister out the door."

"Is that so?" I ask, as her foot rubs my ankle from across the booth. "If you're tired, we can always go back to the hotel and spend the day in bed while our sisters do the spa."

"Tempting, but no." She takes a sip of her coffee, and I get hard just watching her mouth on that white ceramic cup. "You promised me a day out." She puts the coffee down, her eyes never leaving mine. "I'm looking forward to whatever you have in mind."

"You, Jezebel Stuart, are a tease."

"Maybe a little," she says, then pulls her foot away. "But I can be good." She sets her fork down and leans back. She's managed to eat half of her short stack. Which, considering the size of the pancakes, is pretty impressive. "So tell me about this place. How'd you find it?"

"I've been coming here since I was a kid. I always got a kick out of the *Sorry, we're open* sign, and when Kerrie was little, I used to tease her by telling her that the whole restaurant was part of a time warp."

"Because of the sign that says they're open 24/8?"

"She never believed me," I say. "My sister is far too cynical."

Jez laughs. "Yeah, she looked pretty cynical this morning when she was jumping up and down and clapping about a spa day."

"She hides her cynicism well," I retort, and Jez throws her napkin at me.

"When are you going to tell me the plan for the day?"

"Never," I say. "You're just going to have to trust me and go along for the ride. Think you can handle it?"

She crosses her arms and narrows her eyes. "No," she says. But her smile says yes.

Half an hour later, she's already bought Delilah three souvenir T-shirts from Prima Dora, a local shop next door to Magnolia, along with five packs of kitschy cocktail napkins. "Del loves this kind of stuff," she says, grinning as we walk hand in hand, the shopping bag tight in my free hand. "Where to now?"

"Now we wander."

"I like it here," she says after we've walked a few more blocks. "Definitely trendy, but it's colorful and fun and most everything seems local. Oh—"

She stops at the corner and points to Allen's Boots. "*That* I need." Her smile is wide as she turns to me. "Cowboy boots for when I'm back in LA. Authentic ones, don't you think?"

"Who am I to argue?" I say, and we cross the street and head inside. Unlike some of the stores on South Congress, Allen's Boots has been in this location forever, and the guys in there know what they're doing—even going so far as to tell Jez that she'll be better off if she breaks the red boots she's chosen in slowly. She, however, insists on wearing them for the rest of our jaunt.

"I like them," she says, kicking her foot out as soon as we're back outside in the sun. She does a sort of hop-step, then leans against me as she laughs. "I saw that in a movie once. Well, not *that*. But some sort of dance step."

"We'll start with the two-step and let you work your way up."

"You know how?"

"I've managed once or twice."

"Show me," she insists, taking my hands as if we were waltzing.

I laugh and back away. "Trust me. It's better if I don't try to teach you in public. My skills aren't that good."

"On the contrary," she says, letting her hand slide down my T-shirt, and pausing just below my belt. "I think your skills are excellent."

"Jez..."

I'm sorely tempted to blow off the rest of our excursion and teach her a few horizontal dance steps. But she just laughs and skips back. "Later," she whispers. "Promise?"

"Oh, yeah," I assure her.

She takes my hand and we head down the street again, and we talk about everything and nothing. The knickknacks in the windows, the shoppers passing by. The weather. Books. Even Irish poetry, although how we got on that subject, I have no idea.

When I ask, she just shrugs and laughs and grabs my hand, looking more carefree than I've ever seen her. And right then, I think that there's not a single thing I want more in the world than to keep her looking that way forever.

It's a dangerous thought ... but somehow, it's not as terrifying as it should be.

"Thanks," she says later, as we leave Lucy In Disguise with Diamonds, both sporting funky pairs of retro sunglasses. "I needed this."

"Who doesn't need neon sunglasses?"

"Good point," she says. "But not what I meant. Seriously," she adds, putting her hands on my shoulders and rising up on her tiptoes to brush a soft kiss over my lips. "Thank you."

She starts to pull away, but I cup her head, and keep her

close, deepening the kiss until she moans, and I feel the reverberations all through my body.

"Where to now?" she whispers.

"Well, I have a whole day planned. After SoCo, I thought we'd rent a paddleboat and spend an hour or so on the river. Then we could grab lunch at one of the food trucks on Barton Springs Road, then head to South Austin and check out the Wildflower Center before heading back downtown for a sushi happy hour."

"That sounds amazing."

"Or we could skip all that, and I could show you my favorite view of the river."

"Where's that?"

"My condo."

Her eyes widen almost imperceptibly. "So, I'm guessing that the view of the city is a euphemism?"

"It might be," I admit. "I know you said you wanted your day out. But Jez—"

"Shut up, Pierce," she says, silencing me with a finger on my lips. "And let's go. I'd hate to miss an exceptional view."

CHAPTER ELEVEN

IT'S A GORGEOUS MARCH DAY. The afternoon sun sparkles on the river. The trees are green, a few of them even starting to bud.

It's truly a beautiful view.

None of that, however, compares to Jezebel.

We're in my living room, and she's at the window that opens onto the balcony and overlooks the scenic river view. But it's the woman who truly takes my breath away.

She's already taken off her boots, but now I want to do away with the rest of her clothing, and I step up behind her, determined to make that happen. "Close your eyes," I say, and I'm gratified when she does. "Arms up." Once again, she complies, and her willingness to trust me is as much of a turn-on as her soft skin and delicious scent.

I grab the hem of her shirt and pull it up over her head. She makes a little whimpering sound, but doesn't object.

"Next the jeans," I say, as I peel the bra off of her and toss it aside. "Take them off for me. Underwear, too."

The windows are slightly tinted in defense against the sun, and at this time of day, there's a bit of a reflection. She looks up, then meets my eyes in the glass. I wait for her to protest, but she says nothing. She just unbuttons her fly, then wriggles out of the jeans, her underwear slipping down with the denim.

Then she stands there, looking out at this wild section of Austin, her hands at her sides, her legs slightly parted.

I'm standing behind her, but in the window, I can see that her nipples are tight, and she's biting on her lower lip.

"This excites you," I say, and when she nods, I exhale with relief. Because damned if it doesn't turn me on, too.

"This is my favorite view," I say. "Not the city. Not the trees. Not the river. But you standing in front of me, your skin glowing, your body reflected in the window. Because honestly, how could anything be more lovely?"

"Liar," she says, her mouth curving into a smile. "Nice words, but they're a lie. How can this be your favorite if you've never seen it before?"

I step up behind her and cup her breasts, then slide one hand down between her thighs. She's wet—so damn wet— and all I can think is *mine*.

"I've seen it before. Not specifically, but the idea of it. The idea of you. An innocent beauty standing right in front of me, naked and wanting me." I move the hand on her breast up to her forehead so that I can bend her head backwards, elongating her neck. She draws in a shaky breath, but doesn't move. "Tell me you want me."

"Yes. So much."

I release her, and she sighs, but stays like that, leaning backwards against me, so that I'm supporting her weight and she's trusting me to keep her upright.

One of my hands is still between her legs, and I tease and stroke her until she's writhing against me, hot and ready. "Take off your clothes," she demands.

"Anything the lady wants," I say, as I hurry to strip.

"Do you mean it?"

I tilt my head, wondering what she has in mind. "Try me."

She slides into my arms, kicking away the last of my clothes, then captures me in a white hot kiss that both surprises and excites me. "Jez, baby," I say, when I pull away, gasping for breath. But she's not giving me a break. Her hand slides between our bodies and she strokes me, making me even harder than I could have imagined, and sending a wild heat coursing through me.

"Now," I say. "Dammit, Jez, I need to be inside you now."

"What floor are we on?" There's a frantic note to her query.

"The twenty-seventh."

"Can anyone see in?"

"I don't know. I don't think so."

"The window," she begs. "Please, take me by the window."

Hell, yes, I will.

"Hands on the glass," I order. "Bend over."

She does, and the view is so hot, I almost come right then. But I want to be inside her. I want to be with her. *Her.* Not just sex, but Jez. And as I move behind her—as I slide my cock deep inside her hot, wet, pussy—as I claim her once and for all—I can't help but wonder what that means.

But right now, I'm too fired up too care. Too lost in passion. Too lost in the waves of pleasure rippling over me.

Most of all, I'm too lost in Jez.

And when she explodes in my arms—when she cries my name and shakes so hard her legs give out—I feel like the most powerful man on the earth.

We've sunk down to the carpet, and I rouse myself long enough to clean us up and get robes. Then I open the door and lead her onto the balcony, settling her on the oversized chaise lounge before I go back inside for two glasses of bourbon.

I'm tending her—and that's a far cry from my usual routine.

But it feels right. Good, even.

And when she smiles up at me as I hand her a glass, it also feels remarkably like home.

"I love this," she says, before I can think too hard about these errant, semi-domestic thoughts skittering through my mind. "Way up in the sky with a balcony. It's like living in the city, but still getting away."

"It is," I say. "I'd like to have a house one day, but only if it has that getaway quality. And that would mean a pretty big yard. And I don't have the time to deal with it."

"You could hire someone."

I shake my head. "Not the same. There's something primal and personal about a yard. What?" I say, catching her look of surprise.

"It's just that I've always felt that way. I want a garden, and I don't have one for the same reasons. No time to deal with it and I don't want someone else tending what's mine."

I nod, thinking how much we have in common, and how unexpected that is.

She sighs, and takes a sip of the bourbon. "This has been a great few days," she says. "And to be honest, I haven't had a lot of fun lately," she says. "So thank you."

"Because of the scandal?"

"Yeah. But even before that."

I turn toward her, remembering our conversation last night. "You're living a shadow life."

She bristles. "I love my sister."

"I'm not saying you don't. But you need to live your own life. What happens when she's ready to manage her own career?"

"This isn't your problem." Her words are sharp, and painfully true.

Painful because I want to help. I want to pull her into my arms, hold her close, and help her figure it all out.

And damned if I know where I made that left turn, but I did. And now I'm careening toward something with this woman that I don't fully understand. All I know is that it feels right—and that I'm not ready to put on the brakes.

"It is my problem," I tell her. "I don't know why or how or if you'll let me help. But dammit, Jez, you got under my skin. And I can't walk away. Not now. Not without trying."

Her lips press tight together and she holds her eyes wide, obviously fighting tears. But then she pushes out of the chair and hurries inside.

I give her a moment, then follow. She's in the kitchen, the faucet running, her hands clutching the countertop.

"Hey." I put my hand on her shoulder, resisting the urge to turn her around and pull her into my arms, even though that's exactly where I want her to be. "Talk to me."

"I've got this," she says, more to the sink than to me. "I do," she adds, turning to face me. "It's just that sometimes I wish I could hand it all off to someone else. That I could just let go and back away. You know?"

"I do," I say. I take her hand. "Come with me."

She eyes me curiously, but she doesn't protest when I lead her into my bedroom.

"I can't help with Del," I say. "At least not without some research and a few dozen phone calls. But about you handing it off to someone else ... about that, I have a few ideas."

I watch her face. The flicker of interest. The hint of nervousness. "What do you have in mind?" she finally asks.

"Do you trust me?"

"I—"

She hesitates, and in that moment of silence it feels like the ground has fallen out from under me. And fuck, I want to kick myself, because I should not have fallen this hard, this fast. I know better than that.

But what the hell, right? Because all that's going on here is a multi-night stand. And in a few days, she's heading back to LA, and I'll hop back onto 2Nite, and my life will return to stasis.

In the meantime, I have Jez.

And when she nods and says, "Of course I trust you," everything seems sane again.

"Sit on the bed," I order, and when she complies, I go to my dresser.

"What exactly are you doing?" Her voice is amused, but wary.

"Forcing you to give everything over to someone else. Close your eyes. Now," I add, when she hesitates.

She narrows her eyes, but then she complies—and then yelps a little when I put a sleep mask on her, then tighten it to ensure she can't peek.

"Pierce, I don't—"

"Hush. You're giving yourself over. You're letting go. You're putting me in charge. That's the deal. And I promise you'll enjoy it."

She licks her lips, and I hold my breath, afraid she's going to balk. But then she nods.

"Good. Now lay back and put your arms above your

head, wrists together." I'm certain she's going to protest again, so I'm surprised when she complies without argument.

I get on the bed beside her, then bind her wrists with an old tie. The headboard has a shelf on it, and since I don't have a better option, I unplug my alarm clock and thread the extension cord though the loop of the tie, effectively binding her wrists near the headboard.

"Pierce..."

"Yes, baby?"

"I don't know," she says. "I guess I just wanted to know you'd answer."

"Always. Now relax. Just breathe."

"What are you going to do?"

"Sweetheart, I'm going to make you come."

"Oh."

I smile, seeing the way her body tightens just from the suggestion, and then I settle in to thoroughly explore this woman. I brush kisses over every inch of her. I oil my hands and massage her breasts. I suck on her tits. I kiss my way up her legs. And I tell her throughout all of it how absolutely fucking beautiful she is.

I lose myself in her pleasure. In watching the way her skin contracts at a touch. In judging the pattern of her breathing. I want to know everything, and I lose myself in the reality of Jezebel.

And only when she is writhing and whimpering, begging for my touch, do I gently slip my fingers between her legs, then hold her still when she tries to grind against me. "Oh, no. That's for me to do," I say, and then I make it my mission to take her to the absolute height of passion.

And since she actually screams when she comes, I think that I did a damn good job.

I hold her body as it shakes in the last throes of the orgasm, then very gently I take off the mask and untie her hands.

Immediately, she curls up against me, then sighs deeply. "That was incredible."

"The orgasm or letting go?"

"That's a trick question," she says, opening her eyes. "I came so hard *because* I let go."

"Listen to you," I tease. "My star pupil."

She reaches out to smack my chest, but I grab her hand and kiss it. "If you can do it in bed," I say, "you can do it in life."

"Have an earth shattering orgasm?"

"Surrender some control."

I think I've proved my point, but she just shakes her head, then props herself up on one elbow. "You're forgetting one thing. I trust you."

CHAPTER TWELVE

I TRUST YOU.

The words rush through me, warm and satisfying—and scary enough that I force them aside. This isn't about me. It's about her. It's about Del. It's about finding an agent or a manager or a partner—someone who can share the burden with Jezebel until Del's ready to take it over herself.

And that's exactly what I tell her.

"And my point's still the same," she says. "I don't have to get naked with them, but I still have to trust them. And after what happened with Simpson..."

She trails off with a shrug, then shifts on the bed so that she's propped up on her knees. "But you, sir, are taking my problem far too seriously. I'll work it out. And in the meantime, we need to get going."

She nods at the clock, and I curse softly. I'd completely lost track of time. We need to be back at the hotel in just under half an hour. "You're a bad influence on me," I say.

"The feeling's entirely mutual."

Fortunately, my condo is only a few blocks from the Starfire, and soon enough I'm handing the valet my keys

and ushering Jez into the elevator with fifteen minutes
to spare.

She uses her key to access the floor, and moments later
we walk hand-in-hand into her suite—only to find Kerrie
sitting at the table, looking directly at us.

Her brows rise, and I see a smug little smile flicker
before being replaced by her poker face.

"You're early," I say, releasing Jez's hand. "Where's
Del?"

"Remind me never to be a movie star," she says. "Your
schedule totally isn't your own."

"Kerrie…"

"She's on the set. Connor took her. Said you could
relieve him when you got back."

"The set?" Jez says.

"The producers called while we were in the steam
room. I guess they wanted to get started early or something."
She takes a gulp from her water bottle and looks at me.
"Can you take me home before you go? I've got plans
tonight and no car."

"Sure. Grab your stuff." I turn to Jez as Kerrie starts to
shove magazines and a pair of flip flops into a tote
bag. "You?"

She shakes her head. "I need to sort through a few
things here and make a couple of calls to LA." She reaches
for my hand, glances at Kerrie, then pulls it back. "I'll see
you later, though. When you bring Del home."

"Yes, you will," I say. I step closer, then lower my voice
so that only Jez can hear. "You can fire me again tonight."

"Deal."

"I'm ready," Kerrie says.

"Hang on. I want to grab a water bottle." My phone
chimes as I head for the fridge in the small kitchen area. I pull

it out and set it on the counter, looking at the lock screen notification as I open a bottle of water and take a long swallow.

J from 2Nite has messaged you: Back in town. Let's try again tonight?

I'm about to dismiss it when Kerrie calls for me to bring her a bottle, too. I grab one from the fridge, and head back toward the door, then toss the bottle to my sister. "All set?"

"Let's go."

I wave to Jez, resisting the urge to kiss her goodbye. Not because it would be unprofessional, but because I'd never hear the end of it from my sister.

My sacrifice doesn't pay off, however, because the first thing Kerrie says when we get in my Range Rover is, "You like her."

"Of course I do. She's nice. Smart. Competent."

"That's not what I mean, and you know it. You're falling for her."

"No, I'm not," I lie, because I don't want to get into it with my sister right now.

"It's okay if you are."

"Kerrie..."

"I'm just saying that would be good, that's all. I mean, I know that whole thing with Margie messed you up, but I worry about you. Mom and Dad worry, too. They're just never going to tell you. Or if they do, they'll wait until Thanksgiving and Christmas."

Our parents retired to Nevada five years ago, and while we stay in touch, the phone calls tend to be pretty bare bones. But my parents are more than happy to meddle when we're together in person for the holidays.

I keep my hands on the wheel and my eyes on the road. "Like I said, I'm fine."

"Maybe. But one of these days you're going to have to realize that only Margie was the asshole and not the entire female population. I mean, some of us are actually loyal, you know? And I love you, is all."

I sigh. "I love you, too." I hesitate, and for a moment I consider telling her everything and letting her help me parse out this mess of emotions that's tangled in my head.

But then her phone rings, and the moment is lost.

"Hey," she says. "What's up?" A pause, then, "Sure, I'll tell him. Bye."

"What's up?"

"You left your phone at the hotel. Jez called Connor so you wouldn't worry when you couldn't find it."

"Oh, good. Thanks."

"And apparently Lisa tried to reach you," she adds. "When your phone and the office line went to voice mail, she called Connor. She's in town and wants to meet you for dinner. She told Connor she has news. And he said he'll cover for you on the set."

"News." I frown slightly, considering, but I don't have any ideas. "I was just telling Jez about her. She was asking about our work."

"You told her about Lisa and the stalker? Did you tell her what happened?"

I understand the surprise in her voice; I don't often share that I killed a man. "I told her."

"Like I said," she says smugly. "You're falling for her."

This time, I don't bother to deny it.

I use Kerrie's phone to call Lisa back, then drop my sister off before going home to change. All of that takes about an hour, but I still manage to arrive right on the dot to meet Lisa. She's already seated, and she stands up and flings her arms around me as I approach the four-top near the front of the restaurant.

"I'm so glad you could come. I know it's horribly short notice, but I'm only in town today. We came in to see Daddy."

"How's your father doing?" I ask. I haven't spoken to her father in months. All I know is that he's living in Salado now, a small town about fifty miles outside of Austin.

"Great," she says. "He's been doing a lot of renovation work, so business is picking up. He uses your recommendation on the website I made for him."

"Good. That's what it was for." I take a sip of my water, then notice the bottle of champagne chilling in a nearby bucket. "Are we celebrating?"

She nods, looking like she's about to overflow with her news. "But you have to wait until—oh! Derek!"

I turn and see a tall, curly-haired man scanning the restaurant. He smiles and hurries toward us, then kisses Lisa's cheek. And, I notice with approval, he doesn't flinch at all when he kisses her right on the jagged scar, a souvenir of her attack.

"This is Derek, my fiancé."

"Lisa, that's wonderful. Congratulations to you both. Derek, a pleasure." I extend my hand, pleased to find that he has a nice, strong grip.

"Sweetheart, Mom just called me back. I'm going to step out so that I can catch her, and I'll let you ask Pierce. Okay?"

She nods, and he shakes my hand again. "I apologize, but my mother retired to Taiwan, and getting in touch with her can be tricky. I'll be back soon."

Lisa waits until he's out of earshot, and then says, "I know this is a little weird, but will you be our best man?"

I sit back in my seat, shocked and flattered. "Lisa, are you sure? Is Derek?"

She nods. "I wouldn't be here to get married if it wasn't for you. And Derek's best friend is a girl, so she's going to be my maid of honor. Would you? The wedding's in June."

"Of course. I'm honored."

She leans back with obvious relief. "Oh, thank goodness. Daddy will be so excited. How about you? Is there anyone you're seeing?"

"Actually," I begin, "there's a woman I—"

"Pierce."

Lisa and I look over at the same time, and while she looks completely confused by the angry woman stalking toward us, I have a sudden flash of comprehension.

My phone. My goddamned phone.

"Is this J?" Jez asks. Her arms are crossed over her chest as she nods toward Lisa, but her furious stare never veers off me. "Is this the woman you left me to come fuck? How the hell could you? I thought we—*Dammit."*

Lisa's eyes are wide, and I think she's about to ask me what's going on. Instead, her gaze shifts and she calls out, "Derek!"

"I couldn't get the call back to Mom to go through," he says, hurrying forward. He frowns, looking at Jez. "What's going on?"

"Sit down," I say to Jez as Derek takes the seat opposite to where she's standing.

Her eyes flash with defiance. And then, when she looks at Derek, they flash with confusion.

"This is Lisa," I say gently, indicating her and Derek in turn. "And this is Derek. Her fiancé."

"Oh." All the color drains from her. "Oh, God. I'm so sorry. I—I need—"

She doesn't bother finishing the sentence. Just turns and heads toward the exit.

"Excuse me," I say to the couple. "I need to clear up a little misunderstanding."

I hurry after her, finally catching up to her on the sidewalk outside of the restaurant.

"I'm sorry," she says. "I'm sorry and I'm mortified and I really wish you'd go back inside so that I can feel like an idiot all by myself."

"You don't need to feel like an idiot."

She lifts a brow, and I laugh. "Okay, maybe you do. Because you *are* an idiot if you think that five seconds after I leave you, I'd go to some anonymous girl on the other end of a hook-up app."

After fumbling in her purse, she pulls out my phone and hands it to me. "I went to pick it up, and a message flashed on the lock screen."

"I would have deleted it," I said. "Not even answered it."

"I'm so stupid."

I take her hands. "Come inside. We have an empty place. Join us for dinner."

"Why didn't you tell me you had dinner plans? You said you were going to the set."

I explain about the call, and she frowns. "The universe is conspiring against me."

"Or it's conspiring to get you to dinner with me. Seriously. Join us."

But she can't be convinced. "No, really. I just need to be alone."

"All right." I mentally run through tomorrow's schedule. "Cayden's on deck tomorrow. He's taking Del to the studio for that Sunday morning talk show, and then to the set. I'll come by, too, and we can talk."

"That's okay. Tomorrow's an early afternoon shoot. I'll just see you on the set."

I pause, taking in the bigger meaning of those words: *She doesn't want me coming over.*

"Jez," I say, feeling an unwelcome rush of panic. "You understand that tonight was just dinner with a friend. Right?"

She nods. "I know. I do. And I'm not upset about that."

"Then what?"

But she doesn't say, and I'm left with a hole in my stomach and the feeling that I've lost something, with no idea how to get it back.

CHAPTER THIRTEEN

I GET to the set ridiculously early on Sunday, and I'm pacing Del's trailer when she and Jez arrive. They walk in mid-conversation, and Jez freezes upon seeing me.

I stop cutting a path from the tiny sofa to the tiny kitchen. "Jez, we need to talk."

"Oh, gosh," Del says, looking from me to Jez. "I'm going to be late for make-up."

As she scurries out, I take a step closer to Jez. "Please, baby," I say. "Tell me what's going on. Tell me what happened yesterday. Because I get why you were upset when you had it all wrong. But when we sorted it out—"

"But we didn't," she says. "That's what I realized. We didn't sort anything out at all."

I feel suddenly cold. As if someone has dunked me in a vat of ice water. "What are you talking about?"

"I didn't expect it," she says, moving to sit on the sofa. She has her head down, her forehead pressing against her fingertips.

"What?"

She looks up, and I see the tears in her eyes. "You." A single tear trails down her cheek. "I didn't expect you."

I'm at her side in an instant, my arm around her, pulling her close. My chest is tight, because the words she's saying are the words that have been growing inside me. The words I haven't wanted to examine closely at all. But now … well, maybe now I should.

"Tell me," I say softly. "Tell me what you mean."

"I realized last night, when I saw that stupid phone notification. It felt like I'd been sliced open." She sits up straighter, moving out of my embrace. I know it's so that she can look at me as she talks, but the loss of contact feels as painful as a kick in the balls.

"I'm feeling too much for you," she goes on. "And I know you're not looking for a relationship, but when I'm with you—"

She cuts herself off and shakes her head, as if trying to knock her thoughts into place. "I want more," she says simply. "More you. More time. More everything. I want to let whatever this thing is between us grow and see what happens."

The wave of relief that sweeps over me is so intense that I'm surprised it doesn't knock me over.

I know I should tell her that I want the same thing. That I want to let this play out. For however long it takes.

I should tell her that she's brought me back to life. That she's a miracle and a surprise and so damned unexpected, and that I never want to let her go.

I should tell her that somehow, someway, we'll make this work. That I know it can work, because in my gut—in my heart—she's already part of me.

I should say all of that. Instead, I say, "We have three more days."

For a moment, she just looks at me, and I want to kick my own ass for being such a pathetic loser. I want to call the words back and tell her the truth. But the words won't come. I've been telling myself so long that I don't do relationships, that I can't make the words come. Because what if I'm wrong about her? About us?

What if I let her in close, and she rips off my balls? What if I need those three days to figure this all out?

"You're right," she says as she pushes off the sofa. "We still have three days. And that's great." She runs her fingers through her hair. "Yeah. So, I, um, need to go meet with the production team. It's going to be a while, I think. So, I'll see you back at the hotel. When you bring Delilah, I mean."

I stand and reach for her, relieved when my hand finds hers. "Jez, please. I don't mean—"

But she pulls her fingers free. "No, it's fine. You're right. This has been fun, and we have three more days. I was just..."

She trails off with a shrug. Then she leans forward and kisses me lightly. "It's all good, really. I'll see you tonight. And this thing we have. It really is fun. It's great, just as it is. But I really have to go," she adds, checking her watch.

Then she practically bolts out of the trailer, and I drop back down on the couch.

Fun.

What a horrible word.

I'm still sitting there thirty minutes later wondering how the hell I managed to turn what was shaping up to be the best thing that had ever happened to me into complete and total shit in under ten minutes. Honestly, I must have some sort of rare power of destruction, because I think that's a fucking record.

And maybe—*maybe*—if I hadn't kept reminding myself

how much I didn't want a relationship, I would have grabbed hold of this one and clung on so tightly she could never get away.

Fuck it.

I stand up. Maybe I blew it a few minutes ago, but I can fix it now. I'm not entirely sure how, but I am sure that groveling and honesty—and one hell of a nice dinner—will probably be involved.

I'm just about to go find her and start the groveling part of the equation, when the door to the trailer bursts open and Delilah rushes in, her eyes bloodshot.

"Del, what's going on? Is Jez okay?"

She nods. "She's fine. She went somewhere with the producers."

"So she's not on the set?"

She shakes her head, and I curse the missed opportunity. "Then what's the matter?" I ask.

"They're shutting us down. This was it. We just wrapped the Austin shoot."

I sit back down again. "What the hell are you talking about?"

"They just announced it after we shot the final scene. They've revamped the script. Everything that was supposed to happen under the oak tree or outside the stone house is going to be in a cafe. We're shooting those scenes in LA."

"Los Angeles," I say, as if I've never heard of LA before. "When?"

"Travel tomorrow. Shooting starts up again on Tuesday."

"So much for three days," I murmur. "Fuck."

"Please, Pierce. You have to help me."

I look at her, and realize it's not just the shortened shoot that's bothering her.

"What's going on?"

"Levyl's here already. In town, I mean. He's staying at the Driskill," she adds, mentioning the historic hotel that's across from my office and just a few blocks from the Starfire. "I have to see him. Please, you have to help me get in to see him."

"Are you insane?"

She blinks and tears stream down her face. "Please. Don't you get it? I need to see him. He needs to know that I'm sorry—that I love him, but I did a stupid thing. Maybe he won't forgive me, but I have to let him know I love him, and that I always have. And that even if we're not together, I still want to be his friend, and I never, ever meant to hurt him."

"Del..."

"No, please. I know it's a risk. And I know that maybe he'll push me away or tell his people to not let me in, but I've got to try. I can handle the hurt, Pierce, I really can. But I can't handle knowing I might have missed out on something good. And I really can't handle knowing that I hurt someone I love and didn't try to make it better, you know?

I sigh. Because, goddammit, I know all of that.

And I know that this kid has a hell of a lot more courage than I do.

"If this ends up on social media, your sister is going to kill both of us," I say, and in response she throws her arms around me and kisses my cheek.

"Thank you, thank you. You're the absolute best. I'm so glad you and my sister—"

"Come on. If we're going to do this, we should get going. Do we even know if he's at the hotel right now?"

"He is. He always holes up for a couple of days before a concert. Sometimes he'll invite the press or a few fans up, but he doesn't go out. He might party after, but never before."

"That makes locating him easy. What about access? If you call, will he tell you the room number? Let you talk to him? In other words, is this just a question of me getting you to him? Or do we have an element of covert ops happening?"

"Um, I think it's kind of a CIA operation," she says, and I have to laugh.

"All right, then. Let me make a few calls."

An hour later, I've called in a half dozen favors, talked to pretty much everyone I've ever met in Austin, and have managed to track down the band's liaison at the hotel, who put me in touch with the band's manager, a woman named Anissa.

"Levyl and I have been friends for years," Anissa tells me. "And I was around during a lot of the drama with Del. I don't know if Levyl will see her, but I think he should. And I can at least get you in the room."

As far as I'm concerned, that's about as good an outcome as I can hope for, and so Del and I set off for downtown.

I leave my car at the office, and we walk across the street, then follow Anissa's instructions to get to the service entrance that the band has been using to avoid the press.

Anissa's there to meet us, along with the hotel liaison I'd spoken to earlier. "Thank you so much," Del tells her. "It's great seeing you again. But I'm not getting you in trouble, am I?"

Anissa waves a hand dismissively. "If he's pissed, he'll get over it. Like I said, I've known him forever. Trust me when I say this is nothing."

We follow her through a maze of service corridors to the freight elevator, and then finally to the door of Levyl's suite.

"Ready?" Anissa asks.

Del nods, but before Anissa can take her inside, I reach for Del's sleeve. "You're sure about this? If this visit ends up on social media, it could start the whole scandal raging again, especially if it doesn't go well. And if that happens, you might end up off the movie. Not to mention how pissed off your sister will be."

"I get it," she says. "But sometimes you gotta take the risk, you know?"

"All right, then." I release her arm, then step back. "I'll be here. And Del?" I add, as she's crossing the threshold. "Good luck."

Thirty minutes later, I'm pacing the hallway, trying to decide if the fact that this is taking so long is a good thing or a bad thing. Possibly, she's still groveling. Or maybe he's flown into a screaming rage.

But hopefully, they've reconciled and they're catching up. Frankly, I like to think that at least one of the Stuart women will leave this town in a good place.

God, I'm a heel.

I let Jez believe there was something between us because there *was* something. But then when it came down to the wire, I shut down and shut up.

I don't even have the courage of an eighteen-year-old.

And right here and now, I decide that I'm going to fix that.

Because, dammit, I think I'm falling in love with Jezebel Stuart. And it's past time that she knew it.

CHAPTER FOURTEEN

JEZEBEL'S RIGHT inside the door when we enter the hotel suite, and she glares at both of us as she holds out her phone. "What the hell is this?" she demands, shoving the phone between us.

I glance down and see an image showing Delilah and Levyl with their arms around each other, and Levyl pressing a kiss to her temple.

It's posted on Levyl's Instagram page, and the caption reads *Love this girl. #DelilahStuart #stillfriends #shesalwaysgotmyback #IveGotHers #austintexas #NoHaterz #WeGotThis*

"We made up," Delilah says. "It's all good now. And Jason—the band's new drummer—snapped the picture. Levyl said that if he posted it, the fans would chill out." She takes the phone from Jez and starts tapping and scrolling, a hell of a lot faster than I can manage on my phone.

After a moment, she looks to both of us and smiles. "I think he was right. Everything I'm seeing is all thumbs-up. Nothing snarky or mean at all. Not yet, anyway."

"That's great," I say. "It worked."

"But it might not have." Jez's voice is tight, and I know that I'm going to have to double-down on the apology I came here for.

"Oh, come on, Jez," Delilah begins, but Jez just shakes her head, cutting Del off.

"Go on," she says, pointing to Del's room. And then, when Del hesitates, she adds in a softer voice, "Please. I'm glad it worked out with the fans. And I'm glad you and Levyl made up. But right now, I want to talk to Pierce."

Del looks at me, and I can see the solidarity on her face. If I want her to stay, she's not going to leave my side.

"Go on," I say. "I've got this."

She drags her feet, but she goes, shutting the door firmly behind her. And the second the door *snicks* into place, Jez lays into me.

"What the fuck?" she snaps. "I mean, seriously. What. The. Fuck?"

I lift my hands, trying to calm her down and create a break to get a word in. But she's having none of it.

"I told you specifically that I was trusting you with my sister. And you promised. Not only that, but you entered into a contract. And this is how you live up to your obligations? Seriously? This could have blown up. It could have completely destroyed her."

"But it didn't," I finally manage to say.

Now it's her turn to try to get a word in, but I hold up my hand. "No," I say, taking a step toward her. Which is dangerous, frankly, because right now she looks about ready to boil over. "What was destroying her was knowing that she'd never really apologized to him. That he didn't know how she felt."

I try to draw a deep breath, but it's hard. My throat is thick with emotion. "And once I realized that," I continue, "I knew I had to help."

"How altruistic," she snaps. "Why?"

I look at her face. At those eyes now lit with anger. Eyes that used to look at me with heat. And passion. And humor.

"Because of you," I say simply. "Because that's what's been destroying me."

She turns away, looking down so that I can't see her face. "Don't," she whispers. "Don't even go there."

I hear the vulnerability, and I know I should stop. But I can't. I have to make her understand. Because I'm hollow without her, and I'm so desperate to be filled.

"Just go," she says. "Please."

"I can't." I take a step closer. "Jez—everything you said yesterday—"

She interrupts me with a harsh scoffing sound. "How stupid was I to show you my heart?"

"Jez, please."

"I trusted you. With my body. With my secrets. With my sister and her whole career. I thought you were worth it."

"I am. *We* are. But I fucked up."

"Damn right, you did." I hear the thickness in her voice, and I know she's on the verge of tears.

I step closer. I'm right in front of her now, and I have to force my hands to stay at my sides when all I want to do is touch her. Comfort her.

"I let my past get in the way," I admit. "I thought about Margie and about the way she hurt me. The way she left. But she shouldn't have been anywhere near my head. It should have just been you. Only you."

"Then why wasn't it?"

"Because I'm an asshole."

She lifts her head, her expression wary. "Keep going."

"Because I was scared."

Her brow furrows. "Of what?"

"Of you. Of everything. Of the way you make me feel."

She licks her lips, the anger in her eyes starting to dim. "How do I make you feel?"

"Like maybe I have a chance at forever." I draw a breath for courage. "Like maybe I'm falling in love with you. And I think you're falling with me."

I hear her breath hitch. "Pierce, I—"

"No, let me finish. Jez, I know this has been fast—crazy fast. And maybe we're both wrong, but I don't think so. And I want to put in the time and the work to find out. More than that, I want to make it work. Mostly, I want us to stay us."

A tear trickles down her cheek, and I reach up and gently brush it away. "I was afraid, and I hurt you. And I'm so goddamn sorry. Please, Jez. Please say you forgive me."

She licks her lips and sniffles a little. "Your timing sucks. We don't even have those three days. I'm leaving for LA tomorrow."

I can't help it; I laugh.

Her brow arches up. "That's funny?"

"It's wonderful," I say. "Because you didn't tell me to get lost. All you did was tell me you're leaving. And baby, that's just geography. We can make geography work."

She says nothing, so I take a step closer, then slide my arms around her waist. "Move here. You and Del. You said you want out of LA, right? So come here. Rent a house. Buy a condo. Live with me. But give it a chance. Del's not a struggling actress. She can live wherever she wants."

"She'll want LA," Jez says, and I smile again.

"And she's old enough to live there on her own," I say. "There's this cool invention called the Internet. Texting and video calls and all sorts of magical stuff. And these metal tubes that fly through the sky and get you to LA in only about four hours."

She smacks me playfully on the shoulder.

"You shouldn't hit in anger, you know."

She narrows her eyes. "Maybe I'm not angry anymore."

"Really?" I press a kiss to her jawline. "I'm very glad to hear it. Of course, I still have a lot of apologizing left." My hands cup her waist, then start to slowly slide up, taking her T-shirt with them.

"You hurt me."

"I know," I say, then gently nip her earlobe.

Her body trembles under my hands, and her breath comes out in a shudder. "I think you need to apologize more."

I step back so that I can gently pull her T-shirt over her head. "Sweetheart, I'm going to spend the rest of the night apologizing in every way I know how."

I kiss along her collarbone, then over the swell of her breasts. I tease one of her nipples between my thumb and forefinger, then bend my head to take the other into my mouth, my cock hardening at the sound of her sweet moans of pleasure.

I stay like that, sucking and teasing, soaking in the feel and then scent of her. Then I ease back, releasing her nipple with a wet, erotic popping sound.

I straighten, then look into her lust-glazed eyes. "Enough?" I ask. "Am I forgiven?"

She bites her lower lip, then cocks her head as a tiny smile plays on her lips. "Not even close."

"In that case," I say, as I kiss my way down her abdomen, lower and lower towards heaven. "I'll just have to work a little bit harder..."

EPILOGUE

Eight months later

I'M STANDING in a tux beneath a vine-covered arch at the end of a white, linen runway. Above me, the sky is painted a perfect blue. Behind me, the Pacific stretches to infinity.

From where I'm standing, yards away from the cliff's drop-off, I can't see the crash of the waves against the base of the cliff. But I can hear the roar of the ocean, and I breathe deep, letting the sounds and the sea air settle my nerves as the iconic music begins and the guests in front of me rise from their white, wooden folding chairs.

I look down the aisle, and it's not until I see her that my breath comes easy again. She's walking in time with the music, holding flowers in front of her, looking more beautiful than ever before.

I slide my hand into my pocket and finger the small treasure I've put there. A talisman that I hope will settle my nerves.

Closer and closer she comes until she's standing almost

in front of me. She looks straight at me, then steps off to the side, smiling so broadly her eyes crinkle.

Now she's standing opposite me, and we're like two bookends on either side of Delilah and Levyl, who are holding hands now, their eyes not on each other, but on the man holding the Bible and reading their vows.

They each say, "I do," and the guests start to applaud. And as Levyl and Delilah kiss, the director standing off to the left and just out of the range of the camera yells, "Cut!"

Levyl laughs and swings his arm around Delilah's shoulder as she leans into him. "One of my favorite scenes," she teases, and he bends to lightly kiss her.

They're not dating again, but they've rekindled a strong friendship, and their fans—and the studio—love the continuing *will-they-won't-they* drama. The movie actually came about to capitalize on their renewed friendship, and Del urged both me and Jez to be extras in this movie. Supposedly just for fun, but also so that Jez and I would have a reason to fly to LA for a long weekend.

Over the last few months, we've been spending less time in California and more in Texas. At first, Jez was flying back and forth almost weekly so that she could work with Delilah on the basic management of Del's career. But Del's been grabbing the reins more, both by making more of her own decisions and by choosing and hiring a team to pick up the slack.

"Do you miss it?" I ask as I take Jez's hand and lead her away from the crowd. "Hollywood? The ocean? The California traffic? Handling Dez's stuff?"

"I miss the ocean," she says. "And I miss Del. But," she adds, as she slides into my arms, "I'm very happy with my trade-off."

"You mean the house and the garden," I say, referring to

the central Austin house we bought last month, and into which we've been pouring a stream of money, sweat, and elbow grease.

"Absolutely," she says, then rises on her toes to kiss me. "What else could I possibly mean?"

I grin, then step back, still clutching her hand. "Come with me. I want to show you something."

I take her back to the archway. Nearby, Del and Levyl and Anissa are chatting with Connor and Cayden and Kerrie, all of whom think they flew out for my movie debut.

That, however, is only part of it.

"What?" Jez says, looking around the decorative set piece. "If you're showing me the set, I've seen it already."

"But you haven't seen this," I say, dropping to one knee and holding up the ring that's been burning a hole in my pocket.

Jez gasps, her fingers going over her mouth, and I'm not sure if she's holding back tears or laughter. Or maybe she's just in shock.

"I don't think I could ever find a more perfect venue for a proposal," I say. "And since our friends and sisters are here, I'll never hear the end of it if you shut me down. But that's a risk I have to take. Because I love you, Jez. I think I loved you from the first moment I met you. I love your snark and your heat, your warmth and your sense of humor. You're everything to me. You're my soulmate."

She blinks, and though her eyes are watery, her face glows.

"I never thought I would say this again. I never thought I would want to. But Jezebel Stuart, I don't want to go another minute without knowing that you'll be my wife. Baby, will you marry me?"

My heart is pounding so hard I don't even hear her

answer. But I do hear the applause and whistles. And when Jez pulls me to my feet—when she flings her arms around my neck and kisses me hard and deep—that's when I know her answer for sure.

It's yes.

And as I kiss her back, surrounded by our friends and family, I can't believe how lucky I am.

———

Want more? Don't miss Cayden and Connor's stories in *Pretty Little Player* and *Sexy Little Sinner!*

MEET CAYDEN IN PRETTY LITTLE PLAYER

Bedroom games are fine ... but I need a woman who won't play with my heart.

After years in the military, I've faced down a lot of things, and there's not much I shy away from. Except relationships. Because when you catch your wife in bed with another man, that tends to sour even the most hardened man against women.

When I was hired to keep surveillance on a woman with a checkered past, I went into the job anticipating the worst. But what I found was a woman who turned my head. Who made my blood heat and my body burn. A woman who made me feel alive again.

A woman who was nothing like what I expected, but everything I wanted. A woman who, it turned out, needed my protection. And wanted my touch.

And as the world fell out from under us, and everything I thought I knew shifted, there was only one reality I could hold onto—that the more I got to know her, the more I wanted her.

But if I'm going to make her mine, I'll have to not only keep her safe, I'll have to prove to her that I've conquered my own fears and doubts. That I'm done looking into the past, and that all I want is a future—with her.

Meet Connor in Sexy Little Sinner

It was wrong to stay together ... but we couldn't stay apart.

I've been with my share of women, but none touched my heart and fired my senses the way she did. Her smile enticed me. Her caresses teased me. Her body aroused me.

And yet, it couldn't last. There were too many years between us. A gap we couldn't breach, and we broke it off. No. *I* broke it off. And I've regretted that decision ever since.

Now she's in danger, and there's no one else I trust to protect her. But the more time we spend together, the more I want her back. And all I know now is I have to keep her safe—and despite both of us knowing better, somehow, someway, she will be mine again.

Who's Your Man of the Month?

When a group of fiercely determined friends realize their beloved hang-out is in danger of closing, they take matters into their own hands to bring back customers lost to a competing bar. Fighting fire with a heat of their own, they double down with the broad shoulders, six-pack abs, and bare chests of dozens of hot, local guys who they cajole, prod, and coerce into auditioning for a Man of the Month calendar.

But it's not just the fate of the bar that's at stake. Because as things heat up, each of the men meets his match in this sexy, flirty, and compelling binge-read romance series of twelve novels releasing every other week from *New York Times* bestselling author J. Kenner.

"With each novel featuring a favorite romance trope—beauty and the beast, billionaire bad boys, friends to lovers, second chance romance, secret baby, and more—[the Man of the Month] series hits the heart and soul of romance." *New York Times* bestselling author Carly Phillips

**Down On Me - Hold On Tight - Need You Now
Start Me Up - Get It On - In Your Eyes
Turn Me On - Shake It Up - All Night Long
In Too Deep - Light My Fire - Walk The Line**

Bar Bites: A Man of the Month Cookbook

ABOUT THE AUTHOR

J. Kenner (aka Julie Kenner) is the *New York Times*, *USA Today*, *Publishers Weekly*, *Wall Street Journal* and #1 International bestselling author of over one hundred novels, novellas and short stories in a variety of genres.

 JK has been praised by *Publishers Weekly* as an author with a "flair for dialogue and eccentric characteriza- tions" and by *RT Bookclub* for having "cornered the market on sinfully attractive, dominant antiheroes and the women who swoon for them." A six-time finalist for Romance Writers of America's prestigious RITA award, JK took home the first RITA trophy awarded in the category of erotic romance in 2014 for her novel, *Claim Me* (book 2 of her Stark Saga) and the RITA trophy for *Wicked Dirty* in the same category in 2017.

In her previous career as an attorney, JK worked as a lawyer in Southern California and Texas. She currently lives in Central Texas, with her husband, two daughters, and two rather spastic cats.

Visit her website at www.juliekenner.com to learn more and to connect with JK through social media!

CPSIA information can be obtained
at www.ICGtesting.com
Printed in the USA
LVHW041510111019
633943LV00011B/448/P

9 781940 673967